For my mum and dad
x

Snug in Iceland

Victoria Walker

ISBN: 978-1-7399441-0-0

1

Rachel Richards sat in her boss's office, waiting. She looked out of the window at the crisp winter sky to avoid having to look at the mess on the desk in front of her.

"Rachel, sorry to keep you," Luisa said, as she hurried in, shutting the door behind her.

Luisa Goddard was Head of Development at Snug and never had her door closed. It wasn't a good sign. Rachel thought she was probably about to be fired, although she had no idea why. Maybe the company was in trouble, maybe she'd made some horrible mistake she didn't know about, maybe...

"I want to talk to you about the roll-out programme for Northern Europe," Luisa began.

Their team had been working on the store layouts, fitting requirements and designs for the new stores, down to the choice of lightbulbs for months.

"The launches of the Stockholm and Oslo stores were so successful that we're going to sign the lease on the Reykjavik store next week."

"Oh, that's great news."

Relief flooded over Rachel. Another store opening meant more work and she hoped she'd proved herself enough over the past few years to be an integral part of the plans.

"It is good news. And I hope this will be too...we need someone to oversee the shop-fit, merchandising and launch in Iceland and we'd like you to do it. What do you think?"

Luisa was beaming at Rachel as she waited expectantly for an answer.

"I thought you were going to do that?" Rachel said, realising as she spoke that she could be coming across as ungrateful. "I mean, it sounds great. Thanks for thinking of me. I'm just surprised."

Luisa smiled and thankfully didn't look like she was about to retract the offer.

"Obviously, that side of things has been down to me until now and while we were concentrating on the UK roll-out it was no problem but having the Oslo and Stockholm projects in quick succession has brought things to a head. Realistically, I can't be out of the country for weeks at a time on such a regular basis so we've decided to appoint a Head of European Retail Development and that would be your new job title if you accept."

Rachel thought it sounded pretty amazing. Finally, an opportunity for some business travel with the added benefit of it beginning with a place she had never been to before. And more than that, it meant her hard work had been recognised and rewarded and that felt amazing.

"It means a few weeks at each location, not just Reykjavik but for all the stores we have in the pipeline," she carried on, "but it will be expensed, you'll get an uplift on your salary and you can claim overtime for additional hours, just like when we have a launch in the UK."

"It sounds fantastic," Rachel said, grinning at Luisa. "I'll talk it over with Adam tonight and let you know on Monday if that's okay?"

"Yes, by all means, take the weekend to talk it over but you would need to leave a week on Sunday. I know it's short notice…"

"No, that's not a problem." Adam might be but the sooner the better as far as she was concerned.

"Please Rachel, consider it carefully, it's a great opportunity for you. You're organised," she gestured to the piles of paperwork in front of her, "and there's no-one else in the team that knows the Snug brand image like you do. We need to know that the launches of our first overseas stores are in the best hands, particularly now that we know the model works in Scandinavia. Oh, and keep it to yourself for now, just until you let me know either way."

Rachel got up, opened the door and walked back to her desk in a daze. She had been working hard on the plans for the new stores and thought she might get to help with the merchandising if she was lucky but she'd never dreamed she might be the one to actually run the projects right from the start.

Rachel loved working at Snug. The business had started eight years before as a pop-up shop in Carnaby Street, mainly as a way for the founder, Julia, to advertise a season of artisan craft markets she was putting together. She'd had a vision of what a modern craft market should be like; trying to fling off the 1980s hangover of knitted acrylic tea-cosies, clunky brown pottery and bad paintings that gave most local craft fairs a bad name. She thought a craft fair should be a properly curated group of talented people whose wares complemented each other and exuded an overall feeling of quality and uniqueness that meant the artists could charge a proper price for their work. Her vision was so successful that now there were thirty-two Snug stores across the UK, in all the big cities, while still managing to be an artisan-led company with lots of small designers making beautiful things like cushions, throws, crockery and glassware.

The team that Rachel worked in was responsible for designing the store interiors in line with the brand image. It gave her a huge buzz to see all their hard work come together when a new store opened. In fact, it was easily her favourite part of the job and more than made up for the endless calls she had to make to suppliers and tradesmen for quotes to get the building work organised for each new shop before any of the fun stuff could happen. The promotion should mean that she would get all of her favourite parts of the job with the added bonus of being on-site for the whole project.

"Rach, what did Luisa want?" her colleague, Jess, asked in a loud whisper. "I've never seen the door closed before."

"Oh, we were just going over some of the budget figures for the new roll-out. Luisa thinks they're super-confidential." Rachel pulled a face hoping to convey that she thought Luisa was mad in an effort to put Jess off the scent.

"Yeah, no-one ever cares about the budget," Jess said, settling back to whatever she was doing on her computer.

"Yeah," Rachel said, rolling her eyes at Jess while she wasn't looking because the budget was everything.

Desperate to tell someone and knowing that she couldn't call

Adam while he was at work unless it was a proper emergency, Rachel headed for the ladies' loo with her phone so that she could call her best friend Anna in private.

"Hi Rach, what's up in the land of Snug?" Anna was permanently on alert where her phone was concerned and had answered almost before the first ring had finished.

"I've just been offered a promotion!"

And the kind of reaction that Rachel was hoping to get came down the phone, at considerable volume.

"Oh my God! That's amazing! Wooooooooooo!!!!"

Rachel rolled her eyes, smiling, as she imagined Anna's colleagues thinking she'd gone mad, whooping like that in the office, although they were probably used to that kind of thing from her. Before Rachel moved in with Adam, she had shared a flat with Anna and it was crazy most of the time. Anna was always involved in some kind of drama, usually boyfriend related, that made her life endlessly entertaining.

"Thanks, I was desperate to tell someone, I've only just found out. The first store is in Reykjavik!"

"I've always wanted to go there, that's amazing. Oh my God, you'll see the Northern Lights!"

When they'd started work on the Scandinavian stores, Rachel had made a Pinterest board for each of the cities they were launching in. It helped with planning the décor if you got into the vibe of the place, and she loved her Reykjavik one the most because of the Northern Lights.

"Hopefully. I'm so excited, Anna, I can't believe it. I've spent six years endlessly ringing plumbers and electricians and it's finally paid off."

"You deserve it, Rach. What are you going to do to celebrate? Have you told Adam?"

"Not yet. I'll tell him tonight. Luisa's given me until Monday to decide so I think I'll cook dinner for us. Butter him up a bit."

"Well, just remember it's your decision. I'm really chuffed for you. We'll have to have a night out to celebrate properly."

"Definitely. I'd better go."

Rachel was even more excited now that Anna's enthusiasm had added to her own, so she had a quiet little dance around the ladies' then composed herself and went back to her desk. She googled

'Reykjavik Northern Lights' and found a plethora of companies offering Northern Lights excursions. Looking at the images gave her goosebumps. She couldn't believe she was going to get the chance to actually go there.

The only slight problem was going to be telling Adam.

2

Rachel called into Little Waitrose on her way home and picked up a ready-to-cook Thai green chicken curry and a more expensive bottle of red wine than she would normally buy. Cooking Adam his favourite meal and plying him with good wine might help her cause.

She was always home first, especially lately, because he was working long hours on an important deal which was just coming to fruition. She'd taken to eating alone rather than wait for him to come home only to find that he'd eaten at the office anyway. But tonight, she'd felt the need to pin him down so in the end had sent him a rare daytime text which, even more rarely, he'd responded to, saying he'd be home at 8 pm.

Resisting the urge to change into her pyjamas, Rachel decided on jeans and Adam's old university hoodie; he thought she looked sexy in it which could be useful later. Anything fancier than that and he'd know there was something up straight away. Besides, their loft apartment was open plan and had insanely high ceilings so despite it being a very stylish place to live, in the winter it tended to be freezing. It was in a converted warehouse in Shoreditch and Rachel loved it. Because there was such a lot of floor space, they had huge comfy sofas which she had filled with gorgeous cushions from work. In daylight, it was wonderful when the sun streamed in through the original-paned floor-to-ceiling windows but at night, it was more of an effort to make the place feel warm and cosy.

Rachel eyed up the new bottle of wine that was open and waiting on the breakfast bar, along with the candles she was going to light as soon as she heard Adam's key in the lock. It seemed bad form to open the wine before he got home so she opened a different, less fancy bottle and sipped on a glass while she prepared the dinner.

He was twenty minutes late which was no surprise; Adam was the definition of a workaholic and often lost track of time when he was engrossed in something. No stranger to working long hours herself, Rachel had some sympathy but gradually she had ended up working more and more to fill the endless hours while Adam was still at work and she knew she had Adam's approval and respect because of it even if he didn't behave in a way that made her feel that he deserved the same.

Despite living together, they mainly spent time with each other when Adam had the time and that wasn't very often, so Rachel felt like it should make no difference to him if she was away for a while. He didn't see that that was how it was between them, yet here she was waiting until it suited him to turn up. Again.

Hearing him come to the door, Rachel fumbled with the matches and managed to light the candles just as he walked in.

"Rach, I'm sorry I'm late. I got caught by Steve on my way out of the office," said Adam, as he pecked her on the cheek before he took his black wool coat off, threw it across the back of the nearby sofa and sat down.

He took his glasses off and kneaded the bridge of his nose between his fingers, looking tired and a bit more stressed out than he normally did.

"It's okay, I've just about got dinner ready."

He hadn't mentioned the candles and had just reached for the wine and poured some for himself without noticing how fancy it was. Rachel tried not to be annoyed that he'd not picked up on her efforts.

"God, what a day. The shit has hit the fan with the Scramble deal. Something came up last night so we've been video conferencing with the US all day. I almost called you because I thought I'd be there until late but it's on hold now until Monday." He put his glasses back on. "How was your day?"

"Good, thanks. Better than yours by the sounds of it."

He smiled at Rachel, his deep brown eyes finally brightening as he raked his hand through his thick dark hair to push it off his forehead. Then his face dropped. "What's with the candles? Christ, is it our anniversary?"

"No, no, I just thought it'd be nice to have dinner together. Call it date night if you want. I had a really good day, so you know, it's a mini celebration."

She should have just said it. What's with the candles? I got a promotion! It would be over by now. Now she'd missed her cue and she wasn't sure Adam was in the most receptive mood anyway. She turned to the hob, pushed the chicken around the frying pan and stirred the rice, waiting for him to ask what they were celebrating.

"Oh right. Date night, good idea."

He did sound tired. Maybe she should leave it until tomorrow.

"And what are we celebrating?"

"I got a promotion," she said, aware that it was a complete change of tone from when she'd announced it to Anna earlier on. Adam's indifference to her obvious efforts had taken the edge off her enthusiasm along with her uncertainty that he would think it was as great as she did. She turned the curry down to a simmer and sat down opposite him.

"Wow," he said, "that's great. What's the job?"

"It's Head of European Development. Basically, Luisa doesn't want to carry on doing the European roll-out so she wants me to take over. I know it needs a bit of consideration because of the travelling but it's such a great opportunity."

She paused to gauge Adam's reaction but he just looked blankly at her so she carried on.

"The next store is in Reykjavik so I'd be away for a few weeks. I'd probably be able to come home at weekends, I mean, it's not that far away. Only a three-hour flight"

Adam sat back, nudged his glasses up, sighed and looked at her with sadness in his eyes.

"Christ, Rachel, it's a big deal. I know it's a great opportunity for you, but it sounds like you'll be away a lot. And what happens after this roll-out? You go back to your old job?"

"No, I mean that'd be my job and after this phase of the roll-out, there would probably be more across Europe, depending on how it goes. I don't know, I suppose when I'm back in London it will be the same as normal, Luisa will still be my boss, but I want to take it. I've worked so hard on the stores here and never get to be on-site until the last minute and I've never been to either of the

Scandinavian stores. The best thing about this is that I'll be there for the whole thing."

She watched him cautiously, then bit the bullet and asked, "What do you think?"

"What can I say? It has to be your decision but a few weeks at a time is a lot of time away, Rach. It's wishful thinking to talk about coming back for weekends. Retail doesn't stop at the weekend, you know that."

Adam was right about that, but his lack of enthusiasm was prompting her to start thinking of ways she could start convincing him, and *that* made her realise that she had already made the decision. She looked down into her glass trying to think of something to say that would convince him, a good enough reason she could give to bring him around to her way of thinking.

"Rach, the rice…"

She jumped up and neither of them said anything else until she'd finished cooking and dished up.

"Thanks, it smells great,"

"I do want to take it, Adam. Once I've overseen this roll-out and whatever else is in the pipeline over the next couple of years, I'll be in a great position to move to a bigger retailer."

Despite what she'd just said, she had no major ambitions to be a high-flyer at a bigger company but she thought Adam was more likely to get on board if she said that it would be good for her career prospects than with any other argument she could make.

"If I don't take the promotion, I will regret it, I know I will and I don't want to end up missing this chance. And I'm the best person on the team for the job. I'm not sure I could carry on working on the team if I turned it down and had to work for someone else."

As she spoke, it became clear to her that she was going to accept Luisa's offer.

Adam put his fork down and leant back in his chair. "Look, I don't want to stop you or ask you not to take it, but it does change everything. It could put back our plans for having kids, getting married."

"None of that is happening now, though. By the time I've got fed up with all the travelling, I'll be ready."

Adam was ready now. That was part of the problem. He was where he wanted to be with his career and that was the difference.

He was a senior associate in the mergers and acquisitions department at the City investment bank, Grainger Jones, and settling down properly was the next step for him. They had been together for two years and had been living together for most of that time, so to some extent, it was inevitable. But for all his talk of getting married, he hadn't actually proposed.

"Do you still want all of that with me?" Adam asked.

"Of course I do but I don't want to regret anything. The whole reason I even have the chance is because Luisa doesn't want to be away from her kids. I need to take the opportunity before I feel like that too."

His hand squeezed hers and he reached up and stroked her cheek.

"Sorry, Rach. I don't mean to sound like it's not brilliant, I'm happy for you, I'll just miss you."

"I'll miss you too, but I think it will be good for us to miss each other, don't you? I mean, sometimes we only see each other because we sleep in the same bed."

"I didn't know you felt like that, I thought we were doing okay?" He looked hurt. Maybe he hadn't noticed that they had fallen into a relationship rut and if she was being honest with herself, perhaps that was the reason why she wanted to take the job. She wanted something to happen in her life, something new and something that she could be proud of.

"We have been doing okay, I suppose I think a change wouldn't hurt," she added more softly.

"Change? What does *that* mean?"

Rachel could tell by Adam's tone, by the way he almost spat out the words, that they were in danger of veering into a serious argument.

"It just means that the way things are at the moment can't be how things are forever. I'm not going to be a wife who does a day's work and then sits at home waiting for you alone." Like I do now, she was tempted to add. "Or puts the kids to bed before you get home, while your life stays exactly the way you want it."

She was momentarily surprised by how easily her vision of their future spilt out. These things which had been almost subconscious thoughts until now.

Adam sloshed the last of the wine into his glass, downed it in a couple of gulps and stood up.

"I thought we were in a relationship that we both wanted. I thought we had a future together and now you're fucking off to Iceland. There's no need to pretend it's going to improve our relationship. If I've been holding you back, Rachel, feel free to go."

He walked over to the stairs and headed up to the bedroom.

Rachel finished her meal alone. She'd chosen the wrong moment. He was tired, having trouble at work and she should have waited. But why? She didn't need his permission. But she wanted his blessing and she wanted to share the excitement and triumph of her achievement with someone who could be truly happy for her.

Rachel blinked back the tears. She wasn't upset so much as angry and frustrated. If it had been the other way around she liked to think she would have been pleased for him and excited because he was excited. Maybe if she hadn't brought up that she thought a change might be good for them, they could have left things with him being pleased for her. It was her fault that things had come to this. She was terrible at sensing when she was winning an argument and leaving it alone at the right time.

She sat on the sofa, mindlessly watching the television, more resolved than ever to take the job. The regret she knew she would feel if she passed on the opportunity was almost tangible and she also knew she would always blame Adam if she let that happen.

The job was hers and she couldn't wait to get to work on Monday and accept it.

3

The next morning Rachel woke up first. It was Saturday, thank goodness. Adam was sound asleep still, making little snoring noises. She was glad that he wasn't awake yet; she wasn't quite ready for another confrontation, unsure whether he would be ready to make up or if it would be another argument, so she quietly gathered her clothes and went downstairs to get dressed. After a quick cup of tea, she grabbed her swimming kit and headed to the pool.

There was a beautiful old Victorian pool in Shoreditch where she loved to go. It was never very busy, probably because there were more modern places to swim but it was so atmospheric. The white tiles which lined the pool were crazed with age and there were individual changing cubicles with colourful curtains all around the poolside which made Rachel feel like she had been transported back in time.

She entered the water down the steps which were built into the corner of the pool and made for a much more elegant entrance than having to climb backwards down a ladder. It was cold but refreshing and she knew she'd warm up once she'd done a couple of lengths.

Gliding into her first length of breaststroke, Rachel let the water wash over her head and felt instantly better. Swimming was her thinking time and letting her thoughts wander often helped put things into perspective. This morning she felt she really needed that.

When she'd found out about the promotion, she'd expected it to go down badly with Adam which was why she'd gone to the effort of cooking his favourite meal. He had barely noticed; he was so caught up in his own life and never factored her in in the way that she did for him. Simply moving in together hadn't turned them into a unit, a proper couple in the way she'd expected it to, so it shouldn't have been a shock to her that he could only see the impact on himself of her being away rather than seeing the opportunity it was for her. She'd never dared to hope that she would have a chance like Luisa was offering her now and perhaps Adam had never considered that either. In the same time period, Adam's career had been on a steep upward trajectory and he never asked her what she thought before taking every opportunity that came his way.

It was what she wanted and she was going to go for it. This was her chance. She wasn't going to be swayed by Adam's opinion but what she really wanted was for him to be ready to apologise when she got home after her swim for the way he'd behaved the night before.

When she got back to the loft Adam was still in bed. She made mugs of tea and took them upstairs. Putting the tea down, she undressed and snuggled back under the duvet. Knowing that she was going to have to be the one to make the first move, even though she strongly felt Adam ought to apologise first, she scooched up to him. His back was facing her, he was still asleep. She wrapped her arm around his chest and nestled into his neck. He stirred slightly and took her hand in his.

They lay for a couple of minutes like that, then she whispered, "There's a cup of tea here for you."

"Mmm, thanks."

His voice was full of sleep but he turned around to face her and put his arms around her, finding her lips before he had even opened his eyes.

"Sorry about yesterday," she said, hoping that taking the first step might nudge Adam into apologising too. He needed to say sorry for storming off in the middle of dinner and sulking all night if nothing else.

"S'okay." He kissed her again and then pulled her closer towards him, nuzzling into her neck. The fact that he'd accepted her apology without acknowledging his part in the argument rankled for second but she knew she had to let it go unless she wanted to spend the rest of the weekend with the equivalent of a sulky teenager.

"Love you, Rach," he said softly into her hair as he kissed her more and more urgently. She chose to believe that was his apology.

*

The tea had gone cold but Adam volunteered to make a new pot while Rachel lazed in bed snoozing and when he came back he also brought scrambled eggs on toast, his breakfast speciality.

"Breakfast is served!" he said, putting the tray down on the foot of the bed and managing to get back in without tipping it up.

He reached down and slid the tray up so that it rested in between them. They propped themselves up with some of the pillow collection Rachel liked to have on the bed and which Adam hated. She was tempted to mention how useful they were in this instance but decided against it to keep the peace.

"I'm sorry about last night," he said. "I was surprised that you felt like that about us. You haven't said any of that before."

He passed her the plate and she took a bite of eggs and toast so that she had a few seconds to decide what to say.

"I didn't mean it the way it came out," she said eventually, trying to find exactly the right words so that they could avoid another argument. "I love you but I'm not ready for that next step yet. You've got your career that you love and I know you have to work hard but you enjoy it and if you didn't you wouldn't put in so many hours. I don't begrudge you that, I think you're really lucky. But if we settle down and have kids now I will feel like I missed out on having a chance that *my* career could be amazing too."

"It just sounded last night that if you take the job it means you want to take a break from us."

"I didn't mean it to sound like that. I didn't mean we should literally break up but it will be a break from each other and maybe it will be a chance for us to realise that we miss each other and hopefully we'll be wishing we're together while we're apart." She took a mouthful of the scrambled egg before she carried on, "It sounds weird, but I'm looking forward to it."

"Well, I can't say I'm looking forward to it, coming home to an empty house won't be much fun and the weekends will be rubbish," he mumbled with his mouth full.

"Adam, I come home to an empty house almost every night! Some weeks you just come home to sleep."

"You know what I mean," he said giving her a playful shove. "You *will* miss me you know." He put his tea down and leaned with one elbow propped on the pillows while he looked at Rachel. "I know I work long hours but if I don't, there are plenty of people who would happily work that many hours, do just as good a job as I can and probably for less money. Just because I'm head of the department it doesn't mean I can take it easy."

"I know. I just wish you were around more so we can spend more time together. I miss how it used to be."

She affectionately rubbed his stubbly jaw with her hand.

"It won't necessarily be like this forever. Work, I mean. It's just a particularly bad time. It can be great too and those times make up for the stress and the long hours."

"I want to take the promotion because I think then things could be great for me too. I think it will be amazing, but I need you to think it's okay too. What do you think? Really."

"Of course I think you should take it." He took her hand and looked at her, his eyes full of sincerity. "Just come back to me."

4

On Monday morning Rachel got to work slightly earlier than usual, despite leaving the loft at her normal time. She had found herself inadvertently powerwalking in anticipation of accepting the job offer but when she arrived, Luisa wasn't in her office. Rachel had butterflies in her stomach, desperate to let her know what she'd decided. She turned her computer on, went to make a coffee and saw Luisa coming through the door on her way back.

"Morning Rachel, would you be an angel and make me a coffee too and then we can have a chat."

Rachel took both coffees into Luisa's office and perched on the edge of the chair,

"Oh, thanks, that's great," Luisa said, sliding one of the coffees over the desk towards her. "I thought I'd never get out of the house today. I left Phil to it in the end. Anyway, first things first. Have you had a chance to think about the job?"

"I haven't thought about anything else. I'd love to take it."

"That's fantastic, Rachel! I can't tell you how relieved I am! Congratulations!" She came around the desk, hugged Rachel and kissed her on both cheeks. "And Adam was okay with it?"

Rachel shrugged. "We talked it through. He's really pleased for me."

"Right. Say no more. I can still remember Phil's face the first time I told him I had to go away for more than a couple of days. For some reason it was always a foregone conclusion that if he had to go away there would be no problem, no need for a discussion, even.

Equality still has some way to go, Rachel."

*

Ten days. That's how long she had before leaving for Reykjavik. There was so much to think about and organise for work, that Rachel hadn't had time to think about what she would have to sort out for herself before she left. All she had so far was a Reykjavik guidebook that Adam had bought her when they'd gone to Foyles on Sunday, and her project folder.

Googling 'Reykjavik weather February' completely freaked her out; it was typically minus three degrees Celsius and very likely to be snowy and she had no clothes for that kind of climate. Her winter coat was a vintage wool tweed, entirely unsuitable for getting snowed on, so after work, she dragged herself out to buy Iceland appropriate clothes. Ideally, she wanted to get everything from one shop but being an outdoor shop virgin, she had no idea where to start. Uniqlo definitely sold cosy down coats and thermals so that was where she started. For the essentials like waterproof trousers and snow boots, she had to bite the bullet and go into an actual outdoor clothing shop which made her feel like an imposter.

A couple of hours later, it had been a complete success. Rachel dragged herself home with her many well-stuffed bags, wondering how she was going to pack such bulky clothing into her case.

Adam was working on his laptop at the breakfast bar when she walked into the loft.

"Is pasta bake okay for tea?" he asked, barely looking up from the screen as Rachel went over, draped her arms around him and kissed him.

"Yeah, great. Can I show you my haul?" She nibbled his ear until he turned to kiss her back.

"Go on then. Give me a fashion show."

"I won't put it all on, just the coat and boots to give you an idea," she said putting the coat on, pulling the hood up and doing the zip right up to her chin. Then she put the snow boots on and stood back with her hands in her pockets, absolutely roasting hot. By this time, Adam had turned back to his work.

"Look!" she insisted.

He leant back on the chair with his hands behind his head,

looking amused. "You're clearly well equipped for sub-zero temperatures," he said as he began to rifle through the packets of thermal underwear she'd plonked on the table. "Will you need snow boots if you're in town all the time?"

"I don't know, it's best to be prepared. It will be snowy, I googled it."

"Yes, but when it snows here it hardly ever settles in London. Maybe it's the same in Reykjavik?"

"Well, maybe, but I'd rather be safe. Anyway, they're really cosy so I'll wear them even if there's no snow because it's going to be freezing."

He pulled her towards him, wrapping her puffy cocooned body in his arms and kissing her. "You look the part even if you don't look like my usual Rachel. I guess White Stuff don't do a snow range."

"No, they don't but I think this is quite fetching, don't you?"

"Oh, God yes. Especially the thermals. I wouldn't mind seeing more of those later."

"You are so cheesy."

"But adorable?" he whispered, barely taking his lips away from hers.

"Mmm. Completely," she murmured back.

He pulled away. "I need to finish checking this document tonight." And the spell was broken.

In the absence of anything else to do, Rachel decided to ring her mum and dad. She hadn't told them about her promotion yet and she ought to tell them she'd be leaving the country for a few weeks.

Rachel's parents were great and she enjoyed spending time with them but they didn't understand her relationship with Adam. They liked him and she knew they appreciated that, in their eyes, he looked after her but they thought they should be getting married and settling down 'properly'. 'You are over thirty, Rachel. I was talking to Mrs Busybody at WI and her daughter can't get pregnant and she's the same age as you.' That's the type of conversation she had with her mum. All the time.

Her older brother, Ben and his wife Lucy had her nephew, Albert (Rachel called him Bertie; they didn't) two years ago, so she'd thought that would take the pressure off her to provide a grandchild but as they lived in Canada, her mum and dad didn't see much of Bertie so it didn't help. It also didn't help that whenever she decided to visit her parents, Adam more often than not couldn't make it, which didn't go down well with them. It didn't go down brilliantly with her either and she ended up defending him when really, she agreed with her parents that he ought to make the effort once in a while.

Occasionally they would come to London to stay but because her dad was still working they could only come at weekends and were not impressed that Adam always had some work to do or something work-related to attend even though he had 'visitors'.

So, Rachel rang her mum and explained about the promotion.

"Alan! Rachel's got a big promotion at work!" she yelled, while Rachel was still talking. "Oh, your dad's so pleased, love, well done! We're so proud of you."

She then carried on about something marvellous Rachel's brother had done recently; he was always their more impressive child. Then she went into great detail about the last time she had 'spoken' to Bertie, the most incredibly gifted two-year-old in the world and Rachel hadn't realised that her mind had wandered until...

"I know! I'll come up and spend a couple of days with you before you go, sweetheart," she said, and before Rachel could protest, she started shouting again, "Alan! I'm going up to London for a couple of days to see Rachel this week, we haven't got anything on have we?"

Rachel could tell her mum didn't even have the phone to her ear anymore to hear her objections but could hear her dad shouting back that no, there was nothing on the calendar.

"Yes, that's fine love," she said, "I'll come to you."

"Mum, I'm really busy at work getting ready for the trip because it's only me going, so there's loads to do. I won't have the chance to have any time off if you come and I'll be working late every night this week." She felt guilty but it would be so stressful trying to entertain her mum when she had so much on. "Why don't you come and stay once I get back because I'll be able to take a few days off then and we can spend some time together."

"Alright, yes that's fine," her mum said in a pinched, uptight voice that meant it wasn't fine at all, but Rachel wasn't going to back down.

"I'm really sorry, Mum, I did want to visit but I'm just not going to be able to fit it in."

"No Rachel, work must come first. Speaking of work, how is Adam? Is he happy about you going off to Iceland?"

She was still cheesed off, Rachel could tell, but she wasn't going to rise to it. They were very much alike when it came to an argument; both of them had difficulty letting things go.

"Yes, he's really pleased for me," Rachel said. Not entirely a lie now, she thought, also deciding not to mention that he was probably going to visit her in Iceland at some point, just in case it put any ideas into her mother's head. Her parents were big fans of a city break, she was just hoping that Reykjavik wasn't on their radar.

In need of a pick-me-up after the call to her parents, she decided to ring Anna to let her know they'd have to wait until she got back for their next night out.

"Oh, for God's sake Rachel. How busy can you be? Every evening, seriously? I thought we were going to celebrate."

"Well, there's a lot to do. I've been working late and I'm just a bit stressed out with it all. I'd enjoy it more if we could get together when things are back to normal. I'll be back in three weeks."

It sounded pathetic even to her. The fact was, she didn't have a good excuse, she just couldn't face something else to fit in before she left.

"Still too busy even if it's an all-expenses-paid evening out at an up-and-coming bar on Wednesday night?"

Rachel could feel her resolve disappearing because she loved nothing more than going out with Anna when she was checking out a venue for a new client or attending a celebrity launch of something or other. And Anna knew that was her weakness.

"I suppose I could fit it in."

"Christ Rachel, you caved in quickly even for you! Don't worry. I know I'm not enough by myself to tempt you to come out but I always know what will."

"I am *not* that predictable," Rachel protested.

'Yes, you are but I'm used to it."

They made arrangements to meet each other on Wednesday evening.

"Alright, see you then. And sorry I sounded like I didn't want to see you, I'm looking forward to it. Honestly."

"Oh, God it's fine! I know how you get when you've got a lot on your plate. Even more reason to fit it in. Bye Rach."

As she ended the call, Rachel realised that Anna had picked up on exactly how she'd been feeling over the past few days. She didn't consider herself to be the sort of person who would get stressed out or overwhelmed. Her life, in general, was stress-free but speaking to Anna made her realise how uptight she was feeling. It was because of the time pressure. There were lots of things happening all at the same time but if Anna hadn't insisted on meeting up, all she would be doing for the rest of the week would be working and sleeping and that was not where her life was headed anymore. She was about to embark on a huge adventure and it was about time she started embracing every opportunity that came her way.

5

Rachel was on the tube with two complete strangers pressed against her more intimately than Adam ever was, and for once she didn't mind. It was insanely crowded on the rush hour Piccadilly line train, but Rachel was on her way to meet Anna for their night out and to finally have a proper celebration and she was feeling elated again, for almost the first time since she'd been offered the new job.

She had spent the day finalising her fixtures and fittings list and had pored over the drawings for the new store enough to feel happy that she wouldn't be winging anything in Iceland. Adam was out at a client dinner and wouldn't be in until late and as she marched through the crowds towards Seven Dials, she was glad she'd made time to see her friend.

Rachel could see Anna waiting, enveloped in a very shaggy cream faux fur coat. She was never late which made a nice change for Rachel who spent more time than she cared to think about waiting around for Adam.

"Hi, sorry I'm late," she said as they hugged. "I love your coat!"

"Thanks, I got it at the weekend. Couldn't resist it. And you're not late. Chill."

Anna looked down at Rachel's feet. She was wearing her favourite black patent brogues in sharp contrast to Anna's high heeled knee-high boots.

"I knew you'd wear those clod-hoppers. Hello? We're going to a cool bar, not a student dive."

"They're fine," said Rachel, used to Anna trying to push a more polished look onto her. "They're comfortable and I did have to get the tube over here and walk to work this morning. So where are we heading?"

Anna rolled her eyes. "At least the rest is passable," she said casting her eye over Rachel's floral midi dress and black opaque tights which were visible underneath her coat. "It's not far, just along here. The guy who owns it is being bankrolled by his father and basically, he wants us to put it on the map with the celebrities," Anna explained, as they walked along with their arms linked.

"Who do you think will be there?"

"Nobody." She elaborated when she saw Rachel look crestfallen. "Hello? That's why I'm going tonight. To see if there is any chance we can make it into the place *everyone* will want to go to. Then maybe next time you'll see someone exciting. Although they won't let you in once that's happened." She gave Rachel a friendly shove and grinned at her.

Anna knew she loved the world of celebrities and found Rachel's interest in it an amusing contrast from her own natural cynicism but it didn't stop her from constantly trying to explain the reality to Rachel; that it was all a big PR illusion.

The bar had all the makings of being very exclusive. There was a doorman to open the heavy wood-panelled door for them and it was clearly hoping to rely on word-of-celebrity-mouth because there was no signage at all, just a brass plaque next to the door with the name engraved on it. The windows were glazed with etched Victorian glass so you could see hints of people moving around inside and the lighting was intimately low.

Anna introduced herself to the hostess and they were shown to a couple of stools at one corner of the wide, highly polished bar that dominated the room. Normally they wouldn't have wanted to sit at the bar, but here it seemed that they were the premium seats. There was a barman in attendance immediately, offering to make them the house cocktail. Once he had finished doing a brilliant impression of Tom Cruise in 'Cocktail', he left them with their drinks as well as a bottle of Prosecco in an ice bucket and attended to his next customer.

"Let's have a toast," said Anna. "To you, Rach." She clinked her glass against Rachel's. "It's about bloody time! Cheers!"

They both took a sip of their cocktails.

"God, that's delicious," said Rachel, savouring the drink all the more because it was free.

"So how was your day?" Anna asked, taking everything in around her as she spoke.

"Good, actually. I've broken the back of what I need to sort out before I go. How about you?"

"Pretty mundane today. No meetings anywhere exciting so it's just as well I had this to look forward to. What did Adam think about the promotion?"

"He's really pleased for me." A tiny stretch of the truth but Rachel was in a tricky position because Adam and Anna never saw eye to eye on anything, which left Rachel defending each of them to the other.

As predicted, Anna raised an eyebrow. "Really, he's pleased?"

Rachel nodded with a look of what she hoped was total honesty on her face.

"Well, good. I must admit I didn't think he'd be keen on you being away for so long."

"He wasn't keen on that part but he knows it's a great opportunity for me. And I pointed out that being apart for a while, having the chance to miss each other might make things more exciting when I get back."

"Are things okay between you? You're not looking forward to missing him because you want to get away?"

"It's not been great lately," admitted Rachel. "He's been working all hours because of this huge deal he's been putting together."

It was one thing trying not to give Anna more reasons not to like Adam but she did confide in her friend and as any good friend would, Anna seemed to know the difference.

"It's made me realise that things aren't how they used to be. We take each other for granted but I suppose that happens in every relationship."

"I don't know Rach, I haven't got to that part with anyone yet. I know you love Adam but I think he takes *you* for granted. He's obsessed with his job and makes no time for you. Everything's on his terms. Though having said that, you took some serious persuasion to drop work for tonight."

"Very funny. That's what I said to *him* in a roundabout way, that he lets work rule everything. He said it wouldn't always be like this, you know, he might do something different with work at some point. He thinks he has to carry on while the going's good because younger people are coming up all the time who could take his job."

"That's probably true. It's pretty cut-throat."

Anna was right. You did have to be on top of your game in the City. Even though Rachel hadn't known Adam when he was starting out, he'd told her enough stories for her to know how hard he'd worked to get to where he was now.

"But it's made no difference to him that I'm leaving in a few days, he hasn't suggested doing anything together before I go. Whenever I mention that I'll miss him he just says it won't be that bad because he's going to come out to Iceland for a weekend."

"Well, perhaps he will," Anna said, but Rachel knew she was just saying that to make her feel better, not because she thought he would.

"Perhaps," she said, rolling her eyes and laughing. "This cocktail's going down well."

"A good cocktail is a good start. We probably can work with them, there's definite potential."

She smiled at the barman who had discreetly placed some beautifully presented nibbles next to them.

"He fancies you," said Rachel, raising her eyebrows. "He gave you The Look."

"He did not! Anyway, even if he did it would be unprofessional."

"He's not your client. Go for it."

"I'm not picking up the barman. Anyway, it's easy for you to talk, you've got Adam, even if he is a workaholic. His hair alone is worth the grief."

Rachel laughed. Anna always went for men based on their hair or whether they had a beard. Given what she did for a living, it was amazing that she hadn't met someone completely perfect for her. While most people were relying on internet dating, Anna did at least have chance to meet men in real life, the old-fashioned way and Rachel thought all her talk about hair and beards was just a cover for the fact that she was holding out for someone perfect and actually looks had nothing to do with it.

"It's not all about the hair. It's about the suit, you know that," Rachel joked.

"Sorry, yes. I forgot. The problem is you still need the right man with the right hair to make a suit look good. Although the last bloke I went out with, the one that I met at the champagne bar launch, had amazing hair and a very expensive suit but he turned out to be a complete dick."

"Very hard to tell without actually getting to know them."

"That's *so* true. Maybe I should go out with someone who has dreadful hair just to see what happens and then if he's nice I can make him get his hair done."

"It could be worth trying it that way around at this point."

"Anyway, what is Adam up to tonight?"

"He's out with clients." As usual, she wanted to add but knew that would fill Anna with glee. Anna gave her a look anyway. "What?"

"It just seems that lately, from what you say, he seems to be out almost every night with clients. Do you think that's normal?"

Rachel shrugged. "I don't know, it has been more than usual but I suppose it depends what project he's working on."

"You don't think it could be anything else?"

Rachel sensed that Anna was treading unusually carefully.

"Like what? Oh… I know he's not your favourite person but he's not a cheat," she said confidently. Then looking at Anna, she frowned and said, "Why? Do you know something?"

Anna sighed and looked pointedly at Rachel. "I don't know for sure but since it's come up… You know the other night when I went to the opening of that new rooftop bar by the river, near Tower Bridge? Well, I thought I saw Adam."

"That's not much of a revelation, Anna. He's out around there most of the time with clients. There was probably a group of them. Right?"

"It might not have been him. Maybe I didn't get a proper look."

But Anna knew what Adam looked like. He was tall enough to stand out in a crowd and by being vague, Rachel knew she was trying to spare her feelings. Still, being out with someone, especially if it was work-related, didn't constitute evidence of an affair.

"It couldn't have been then because that night I'm sure he was out with quite a few people. Some clients from America apparently."

"See? I didn't think it was him," Anna said unconvincingly.

"Right. What are we having next?"

"I think there would be signs." Were there any signs? He did go out all the time, sometimes staying at hotels in town to save a late-night journey back to Shoreditch. Was that really what he was doing?

"You're right," said Anna. "There would be signs. Let's get another cocktail from that gorgeous barman."

The conversation with Anna left Rachel feeling uneasy. She really didn't think Adam was that type but on the other hand, he did go out a lot and she always took his word for it about who he was with, mainly because it had never occurred to her to think anything else.

6

On Friday, Adam sent Rachel a text during the day which was such a rare occurrence that to start with she had thought her phone was on the blink and had re-displayed an old text.

Will pick you up from work at 7 pm. Is that too early for you ;-)

He was making fun of the fact that she had been working late so often.

Until at 7 pm, her phone buzzed.

I'm downstairs.

"Shit!" she said out loud, having completely lost track of the time. She picked up her laptop, shoved it into her bag, shrugged her coat on and shouted goodbye to the office cleaner before she ran downstairs.

Outside, Adam was leaning against the wall with his collar turned up against the cold, hands in his coat pockets and his bag slung across his shoulder. He looked up and smiled as she came towards him and then lazily pushed himself upright, leaning down to kiss her. Then he led the way, not towards the loft but in the other direction.

"I thought it might be nice to go out for dinner as it's our last Friday night together for a few weeks." He squeezed her hand and smiled.

"That's a great idea. I'm starving. Where are we going?"

"It's a surprise." He sneaked a look down at her - which reminded her of the way that Hugh Grant looks at Martine

McCutcheon at the end of Love Actually - and then took her hand and marched them both to the end of the street where there was a black cab waiting at the corner.

Adam held the door open and she climbed in looking expectantly at him, waiting to hear where he was going to direct the driver but the taxi started going without him having said anything.

She looked at Adam and he just turned and smirked, looking pleased with himself.

"Relax, Rach! Don't you like surprises?"

She loved surprises and he knew that. Every time there was an anniversary or some reason to celebrate anything, she always hoped that he would spring some sort of surprise on her but it had never happened and Rachel didn't think he knew how, so she was delighted that she seemed to be amid a genuine real-life surprise.

They headed towards the West End and turned off Piccadilly Circus, down Regent Street, stopping on the left. Adam paid the driver and they got out next to a passageway between the shops. Rachel had walked past there so many times and yet she had never noticed it before. Adam took her hand and led the way down the passage which had tiny fairy lights stranded above making it look like a starlit night. They came to a doorway with a rope cordon where a few people were queuing. Adam went to the front of the queue and announced himself to the door person. They were immediately ushered in and asked to hand over their bags for safekeeping. This seemed weird to Rachel but she glanced at Adam and he seemed completely fine with it so she went ahead and handed over her things. Then, a man came towards her and threw what looked like a blanket over her head. It was so quick, that she had no time to react and managed to muffle a tiny scream as she realised that it was a quilted, hooded poncho, not a blanket and when she emerged she could see that Adam had a similar, very fetching poncho on too.

"What is going on here?" she said, looking wide-eyed with disbelief at Adam who just grinned at her.

"Keep your gloves on at all times," said the poncho man and Rachel saw that there were fleece-lined mittens attached to the poncho, a bit like the gloves attached by elastic through the sleeves of your coat when you were a child, "and remember you can always leave if you're too cold."

He moved ahead of them and opened a door which led to a dark hallway, gesturing for them to go through. Adam pushed open the next door and a rush of freezing cold air came out to hit them.

Inside the dimly lit room was ice. Lots of it. There were ice sculptures, walls of ice with beautiful carvings in them, all of it amazingly lit up with blue and pink lights and even a circular bar at the other side of the room, also made of ice.

"Welcome to the Icebar!" said Adam beaming at her, "I thought this would be the perfect place to come to send you off to Iceland in style." Rachel reached for his mittened hands and leaned up to kiss him.

"I've never seen anything like it, thank you, it's a brilliant surprise." She knew she was never going to forget this moment. Adam had completely blindsided her and it meant everything. The uncertainty that had been between them since she'd taken the promotion eased and Rachel saw the Adam she had fallen in love with.

"How about a cocktail?"

They were served in small square glasses made of ice and the real purpose of the mittens was revealed.

There was so much to see. The walls were all made of clear blocks of ice built up like a brick wall with beautiful veins and cracks running through them which looked fantastic lit by the coloured lights. As well as the intricate carvings and sculptures, there were little nooks and crannies to explore while they sipped their cocktails. They took photos of each other along with a few selfies. Rachel wanted to make sure she'd remember it.

It was bitterly cold, just how you imagine it would be inside a freezer and because the air was so still, it felt different from being outside in the cold. Rachel pulled up the furry lined hood of her poncho and wrapped the voluminous quilted fabric closer around her. Despite the freezing temperature, the ice glasses gently began to melt on the rims from the warmth of their lips. The drinks went down far too easily and they went up to the bar for a second one.

"We have this place all to ourselves," Rachel said.

"Well, it's not quite so special with another fifty people in here."

"But you paid for us to have the place to ourselves?"

It was such a grand gesture.

"Yes, only for twenty minutes. It's great, isn't it?"

They went to sit in a nook in the corner which was like a little grotto with furs over the icy seats.

"Adam, it's magical. Thank you so much."

"I love you, Rach. I will miss you so much and I want you to remember this night while we're apart."

"I'll never forget it, it's amazing."

She kissed him softly, lingering there with their lips barely touching and their eyes closed, both drinking in this private, special memory he had unexpectedly created for them.

"A few weeks is a long time to be away from each other," she said, almost to herself as if she had only just realised that she might actually miss him.

She tilted her head back to look at him. He kissed her forehead.

"I'm definitely coming to visit, so it won't be that long."

"Promise?"

"Promise," he said tenderly, then pulled away from her, reluctantly realising that it was the end of their magical private Icebar experience when a steady stream of ponchoed people began coming through the door, breaking the spell.

It was the most romantic evening that Rachel had ever had. She was overwhelmed by the thought and effort that Adam had put into making it such a special night for them before she left, and it made her wonder whether her feelings that he never put any effort into their relationship were unfounded. Perhaps she had just forgotten how things could be when they were good. Maybe the argument they'd had on the night of the promotion was the catalyst for this grand gesture. Every relationship had its ups and downs and perhaps she was guilty of having a selective memory, dwelling only on how things had been recently. But right now, she felt like she had in the beginning and it was brilliant.

They had met when Rachel was on a work night out, quite a rare occurrence for Snug, but Jess had just started working there so they were doing some team bonding. Adam was in what was now their favourite bar having a drink with his friend, Jim. It was relatively quiet, being a weeknight, and the two of them had started exchanging pleasantries while they were stood at the bar together waiting to be served. After that, they both went back to their own evenings but kept stealing looks at each other. Adam always told her that he had loved her sparkly eyes and quirky dress sense; she was wearing an Orla Kiely dress and a very well-worn pair of black Doc Martens. Her dark brown hair was cut in a choppy bob with a big fringe, like Claudia Winkleman's.

Adam was wearing a suit, that's all, but goodness he looked great in a suit. That effect hadn't worn off for Rachel even though she saw him wearing one every day now. He also wore the same glasses then that he did now; very cute, kind of old-fashioned, brown tortoiseshell rim glasses which made him look gorgeous.

On that first night, Rachel had left before Adam and Jim but as she was leaving, Adam had come over to her and asked if she'd like to meet him there for a drink the following night. She said yes, and the next night made sure to be late so that he would definitely be there first – the first and last time that had happened. He was sat at the bar, turned towards the door and when he looked at her and grinned as soon as she walked in, Rachel's legs went to jelly, she fancied him so much. She couldn't believe that he was so attractive and he liked her. They talked and drank for what felt like hours and neither of them wanted the evening to end. Rachel thought at that moment that he was The One.

She still thought he was probably The One. Mainly because she couldn't imagine being with anyone else and although they were a little bit out of sync at the moment, they were meant to be together. Any thoughts that his grand gesture with the Icebar was linked to a guilty conscience over what Anna may have seen were pushed aside.

7

The night at the Icebar had turned out to be their last together before she left. Adam's American clients had insisted that he spend the evening with them at their hotel the following night, which was the night before her flight, and apparently, there was nothing he could do about it.

"I have explained to them, Rach, but with the deal about to be signed, they're insisting."

That had been during his flying visit to the loft after spending the whole of the next day at work, even though it was Saturday. He only stayed long enough to change his suit for something more casual and to grab his overnight bag.

"I'm so sorry. I wanted our last night together to be special."

"Don't worry, it's fine," she heard herself saying. "Last night was special enough to last me for ages." She leant up to kiss him and received a peck in return.

"Love you, Rach. See you in a couple of weeks." Another peck and he was gone.

*

Rachel decided that she had time for a quick cup of tea before the taxi was due to pick her up. The loft was too quiet and she was too excited to do anything while she waited, she just wanted to be on her way. Her case was ready by the front door and she was 'light-layered' to the hilt to cope with the transition between the relatively mild London winter and the proper wintry weather she was expecting in Reykjavik.

It had been such a palaver trying to pack and it had become immediately clear to Rachel that she would either have to wear the snow boots on the plane or forfeit taking any other footwear with her because they took up half the case on their own. She was planning to wear her new coat but even so, she wanted to take a couple of bulky sweaters and at least two pairs of jeans and the boots were compromising that. So, in the end, the snow boots had to be worn and right now, in the mild winter weather of London, Rachel felt like a twit.

After a couple of slurps of tea, the taxi arrived and Rachel immediately went from being excited to nervous as soon as the intercom rang. She buzzed the driver up and opened the door ready.

"Alright, love?" he panted as he appeared at the top of the stairs, "I'll get this case in the cab." He had already grabbed it and was off before she could answer.

"Great, thanks, I won't be a minute," she called after him, putting on her gorgeous plum-coloured coat, then instantly realising that she would be too hot with a coat on, she took it off again and tried to squash it down so she could stick it through the handles of her holdall.

She took a last look at the loft as she mentally checked off her 'don't forget' list, and then shut the door.

*

The flight to Reykjavik was only two and a half hours. Although it was just 3 pm when they landed it was dark outside and, they had been informed by the captain, very cold.

Rachel had decided to book a visit to the Blue Lagoon as part of the transfer to her hotel. It had felt like a risky extravagance when she'd booked it but now she was glad she had because she wasn't tired and was desperate to see something of the country before she had to start working. It also really appealed to her to go there in the dark. There was a man from the tour company waiting in the arrivals hall with a clipboard.

"Hi, I'm Rachel Richards, I've booked a Blue Lagoon visit?"

He had a friendly smile and was dressed in a bright red down coat which was open enough to reveal a traditional Icelandic knitted sweater that looked cosy. He was quite tall, taller than Rachel but not as tall as Adam, she noted, slim with blue eyes, short blonde tousled hair and not quite a beard, but a few days of stubble.

"Welcome to Iceland, Rachel. I am Jonas, I'll be the guide for your visit to the Blue Lagoon today. Our minibus is just outside," he gestured towards the revolving doors, "Olafur will help you load your bags and we will be off as soon as we have everyone." He smiled at her and she felt herself unexpectedly blush.

"Thanks, Jonas," said Rachel and he smiled and nodded in an 'at your service' kind of way.

Rachel pulled on her coat and hat, put her hood up and prepared for the chill. It was very cold. The iciness hit her as soon as she walked outside, just like when you fly to a hot country and are hit by the warmth as you leave the airport but the other way around. It was a stark contrast to London where it had been unseasonably mild when she left, but the air was dry and clean-feeling and she felt instinctively good about Iceland straight away.

The drive to the Blue Lagoon took about twenty minutes. Jonas gave a chatty introduction to Iceland as they travelled and pointed out the very few sights that could be seen in the unusual twilight of the afternoon.

Aside from the fact that it was already dark, the path to the Blue Lagoon was bordered by huge boulders so there was no hint of what to expect from the outside at all. They all followed Jonas inside and waited while he spoke to the receptionist, then they were called forward individually and given a towel and locker key.

The changing rooms were very swanky, like a high-end spa but absolutely vast. There were some signs which alluded to the fact that you should shower naked before you went in and that you should drench your hair in conditioner and leave it in because of the silica in the water. Rachel was dubious about the showering requirements but did take notice of the hair advice.

Standing at the door and seeing the few metres of icy coldness that she'd need to cross to get to the pool made her wish that she'd splashed out the extra and hired a robe but instead, she braced herself and opened the door. It was instantly so completely freezing cold that her planned nonchalant walk to the steps of the pool turned into a flailing run. She immersed herself as quickly as she could, ducking her shoulders under the strange milky-blue water which immediately warmed and relaxed her. She could barely see through the steam clouds and the darkness so she moved around the edge of the pool then settled on an underwater ledge and lay her head back, looking at the darkening sky.

"Would you like a drink?"

She turned around to find Jonas crouched on the side of the pool behind her, now wearing a knitted hat and carrying a tray of glasses.

"It's Icelandic beer, very refreshing."

"Oh, thanks," she said, twisting round to take a glass.

"Are you enjoying it?"

"It's amazing, apart from being freezing before you get in."

He smiled at her and his eyes crinkled at the corners which Rachel thought was nice because that meant he must smile a lot.

"That just makes it all the better when you do get in," he said.

"True. Thanks for the beer." She raised it to him, "Cheers!"

"Skál!" he said and disappeared into the steam.

Rachel was surprised to find herself wishing that he'd stayed to chat for a bit longer. She was probably just feeling a bit lonely, she told herself. It was a lovely place but it would be lovelier to share it with someone special. Not that he was special. He was probably special to someone with eyes like that, but not special to her. Adam was special but he wouldn't enjoy this, he never even wanted to go swimming with her. That was quite a sad thought; that there was no-one who would want to be here with her in a romantic sense. The thought of being there with Jonas lingered uncomfortably for a moment in Rachel's thoughts before she lost herself in the feeling of complete contentment that had enveloped her.

After two hours of bliss in the Blue Lagoon and what felt like another two hours spent trying to wash the conditioner out of her hair, Rachel and the others in their party congregated back in reception. She bought some souvenir mud face packs for her mum and Anna which might well have been extortionately expensive but as she hadn't got to grips with the exchange rate yet, she had no idea so decided that it didn't count.

Jonas did a headcount as if they were on a school trip and announced that it was time to leave. He waited until everyone had headed outside and followed behind, next to Rachel who was walking at the back of the group.

"I was wondering if you would mind sitting at the front with Olafur and me?" he asked. "We have a couple of people who came to an earlier session and then stayed for a meal so we are quite full. I think they are all couples so... normally we wouldn't ask a guest to do that but..."

"It's fine, I don't mind."

"Thank you. It is much appreciated."

Rachel climbed into the front of the minibus behind Jonas so at least she wasn't sat in between them which really would have been awkward. The intense state of relaxation that the Blue Lagoon had lulled her into was now rapidly dissipating as they set off towards Reykjavik. This was it now. The adventure was about to start in earnest and she found herself buzzing with excitement as she thought about what was ahead, mixed with a little trepidation at it being the first store she would be in complete control of from start to finish. But she knew she could do it.

"Have you been to Iceland before, Rachel?" Jonas asked, cutting into her daydreaming.

"No, it's my first visit but I think I'm going to love it if the rest of it is as nice as the Blue Lagoon."

"Well, the Lagoon is wonderful but there are plenty of beautiful things to see in Iceland which you won't have to share with a hundred other people." Jonas grinned.

"I would love to see more but I'm here working, so I'm not sure I'll have much spare time."

"Let me know when you are free and I can arrange for you to join one of our Golden Circle tours. It is a typical tourist thing to do in Reykjavik but it is a good start. You will enjoy it. Then if you do have more time you could go for something more adventurous like a glacier walking excursion." He rummaged in the folder he'd been carrying and handed her a brochure.

"I'm not sure I'm as adventurous as that but the Golden Circle tour looks good," she said, thumbing through the brochure. "Thanks." She couldn't help but think how amazing his English was and how much she liked his accent.

"What do you do?"

"I work for a retailer. We're opening a new store here."

"Oh, is it the empty one on Laugavegar?"

"I think that might be the address actually, yes. How do you know that?"

"Most overseas stores are on that street so it was a lucky guess." He smiled at her, his twinkling eyes hinting at a sense of fun.

"I'm looking forward to seeing it. I've only seen a photo of the shop front so it's always nice to see the rest of the street."

"Your hotel is just one street over."

Rachel wondered for a second how he knew where she was staying but realised that of course he knew. It was a transfer.

They had started to pass more houses, it was becoming more built up the closer they got to the city and the road had turned into more of a motorway. Jonas began to give a running commentary over the speaker system on the sights they were passing. Then, all too soon, he announced that they were almost there.

"In a minute, we will start to drop you at your hotels but first we will drive past the harbour to show you the opera house, Harpa. Some people think it is very beautiful although many people think it is ugly."

Rachel gasped when she saw the large glass-paned building made of a metal, honeycomb type structure that had an amazing light installation across the entire front of the building making it look as if the Northern Lights were shimmering across it.

"It's beautiful," she said. "It looks like the Northern Lights, the closest I have ever seen to them anyway."

"This is a good time of year to see them for real," said Jonas, "but it is very unusual to see them in the city because of the light pollution."

Having started to lean forward in her seat, staring at the sky in the hope of a glimpse of the aurora, she slowly sat back again trying to look as if she knew that obviously, you wouldn't be able to see them now.

"You would need to go on an excursion!" he grinned and tapped the brochure on her lap.

8

The hotel was a modest white building, traditional in style, which from the outside didn't look big enough to be a hotel. It was on a narrow street that was entirely blocked when the minibus stopped outside. Jonas jumped out and unloaded the bags, carrying them up the steps to the door. He held his hand out and when Rachel took it to shake, he pulled her towards him and gave her a quick peck on the cheek. He smelled gorgeous; musky mingled with fresh air.

"Good to meet you, Rachel, I hope you call me about an excursion."

"Thanks, Jonas, I will," she said, slightly surprised by the kiss. She grabbed her holdall and managed to man-handle her case through the door as they drove away.

The hotel had a lovely welcoming foyer which was modern but cosy with a log fire opposite the reception desk and a couple of easy chairs.

Rachel's room was up in the eaves and the receptionist had assured her that she would see glimpses of the sea through the roof windows in the daytime. It had a thick carpet, a huge bed and an amazing bathroom with a walk-in shower and a bath with jets in. All the decor was shades of grey and cream with accents in mustard and reds, very Scandi and very Snug.

She unpacked straight away and then sat on the bed to check her emails. Amongst all the usual rubbish in her inbox was a message from Adam asking her to call when she had settled in and one from Luisa letting her know that she had a meeting at the new store at 10 am the next morning with a man from Reykjavik building control. It seemed like it would be a good idea to suss out where the store was before the morning and besides, it would be a good opportunity to find something to eat. Having had a little taste of the city on the journey, she was desperate to explore.

Rachel double-checked her route with reception and headed outside, shoving her hands into her pockets to find her hat and gloves, then pulling her hood up too. It was hard to imagine how cold 'cold' could be when it barely ever got down near zero in the middle of a London winter, and in hindsight, she thought she might have gone for style over substance with her choice of hat and gloves because she was absolutely freezing.

Opposite the hotel, a narrow cobbled road led uphill to a more vibrant, brightly lit and bustling street which, going by Jonas's description, was Laugavegur. She turned right and headed towards where she thought the shop would be. There were so many interesting stores but it was an inviting looking coffee shop, Te & Kaffi, which caught her attention so she called in for a coffee and something to eat while she called Adam. She ordered a latte and a delicious looking muffin and took a seat near the back of the shop in a dark little corner. The coffee shop was made for romance and clandestine meetings, it was cosy, warm, and lit with old-fashioned pendant lights casting a soft glow over each table.

As there was no time difference between Iceland and the UK, Rachel knew that at 7 pm, Adam would probably be at home having dinner.

"Rach!" He sounded in good spirits and was somewhere very noisy.

"Hi! I just arrived at the hotel!"

"Rach, it's so noisy here, I can't hear you! Let me call you later!" he shouted down the phone.

"Okay... where are you?" she asked, but he had already hung up. Weird. He obviously wasn't at home but he hadn't mentioned that he was planning a night out. Perhaps he was still having to entertain the American clients.

When they first met he was living the life of a single, high-earning banker. He was one of those people who got large bonuses and went on the associated wild, very expensive nights out. Since they'd been together that hadn't happened much, not that Rachel would mind, but it was just the single guys that tended to party like that and Adam preferred not to anymore. He occasionally went out for a drink with his team but these days most of his evenings out were entertaining clients.

She couldn't help feeling a bit cheesed off that he was clearly in a bar somewhere when the night before he apparently couldn't get away from work at all to be able to spend the evening together. A sudden pang of homesickness coupled with exhaustion made Rachel feel sad that he seemed to have time for everything else but her and she couldn't help remembering the conversation she'd had with Anna just before she'd left.

The muffin and coffee were just what she had needed and she tried to forget about whatever Adam was doing and concentrate on being excited to see the new store. It was just four doors down from the coffee shop and had a lovely shop front with a large window, a door in the middle and a smaller window on the other side. She could already picture a living room set-up in the window. It was perfect. Cupping her hands around her eyes so she could peer through to the dark interior, she could just make out the back wall and guessed it probably went back about as far as the coffee shop did which meant it was a great size. She knew the square footage, but even after working with so many new stores, it was hard to visualise how that translated into space. Nick, the build team site manager, who she was also meeting in the morning, had the keys at the moment so without the possibility of looking at anything else she carried on strolling down the road.

As she headed back to the hotel, Rachel made sure to follow the same route so as to not lose her bearings in the dark, although that would probably happen in daylight too at this stage. Everything was so pretty in the dark. There were lots of fairy lights strung in the trees which lined the pavements, and the houses that she could see on the side streets had twinkling lights decorating their gardens as if it were still Christmas time.

A book shop, which seemed to be a coffee shop too, was ahead of her, just about opposite the little side street she knew she had to go down to find the hotel. It looked so welcoming and she could see through the large windows that they sold lots of other things besides books. Five minutes later she had purchased a pair of authentic Icelandic knitted gloves with fleece lining. The outside of the gloves were patterned with bright colours interspersed among the light grey background, reminding her of Jonas's woolly hat.

She walked back to the hotel with a warm feeling of contentment. The adventure had begun and was off to the best possible start.

9

Rachel woke the next morning feeling well rested; she must have slept deeply. She got up and opened the blinds, surprised that at 8.30 am it was still completely dark outside. Having got dressed in all her layers, she went downstairs for a lovely breakfast and by the time she finished at 9.30 am, it was still no lighter which felt very odd.

She was due to meet Nick, the manager of the Snug build team, along with the guy from Reykjavik building control. It was a chance to look over the unit together and make sure everyone was on the same page for how the work was going to proceed.

Nick was already waiting inside the unit. He and Rachel had worked on several of the UK stores together so they were well acquainted.

"Hi, Rachel! Great to see you!" he said, giving her a friendly hug, "What do you think of it?"

They stood just inside the door, surveying the space. It was much as Rachel had seen the night before albeit much brighter now that the lights were on. The ceiling was lower than they were used to in other stores but that would give it a cosy feel. The floor was wooden-block, in a parquet design and in terrible condition but it was being covered with vinyl flooring so it didn't matter and the white-painted walls were pockmarked with holes from previous fixtures, most of which had been removed. Walking through to the back of the store, a staircase led down to a storeroom, toilet and office space.

"It looks good?" Rachel said uncertainly, looking at Nick for his opinion on it.

"Yeah, I think it's in good shape, nothing immediately jumps out as a problem. The fittings you've decided on should all work in here, so yeah, we can start making plans."

He smiled which made her breathe a sigh of relief. It was one thing planning a store on paper, but until you saw the bare bones of a unit, you didn't really know what you were dealing with. Rachel set her laptop down on the old shop counter so that she could start working.

"Let me take the building control guy round when he arrives so you can get on. There shouldn't be any problems anyway."

Well, that flippant comment jinxed it. An hour later Nick and Rachel were shell-shocked. The building control officer had informed them that they couldn't lay any floor covering because the current policy was to restore existing flooring wherever possible. The shop was in the old part of town and they had a programme of conservation and restoration for the older shops. It was a huge oversight on the part of the acquisition team not to have known that this was the case before they took the unit on.

Although it didn't sound like a huge problem, Rachel knew the impact it would have on their schedule. They would have to re-lay the damaged parts of the parquet, then sand and varnish the floor which would look beautiful but that needed to happen first before anything else could even start and it would take longer than they had set aside in the schedule.

Having spoken to the heating and air-conditioning company, they could cope with the delay but the fire alarm people couldn't and would need to come in later than planned so potentially they were looking at a minimum two-week delay.

Rachel's most immediate problem was to sort the floor out. The company they had booked for fitting the vinyl mercifully did provide a sanding and finishing service and they had a contractor who could replace the damaged parquet blocks but as Rachel had thought, it would take much longer and cost a lot more money than the simple floor covering she had planned. Suddenly the whole project felt like it was falling apart around her ears. Get a grip, she told herself after a couple of minutes of sitting with her head in her hands. It was just a schedule change, that was all. She just had to rearrange a few things. There was nothing for it but to just crack on. She needed caffeine and some fresh air but not before she had phoned Luisa.

"These things happen, Rachel, we know that, don't worry. We can save some money elsewhere and we always build a contingency in, that's what it's for."

Luisa sounded so relaxed about it that Rachel could feel the tension ebbing out of her body.

"Time is the main issue. You'd better have a word with the hotel to see if you can extend by a couple of weeks once you know the impact on the schedule."

"Thanks, Luisa. I'll try and get started on whatever we can in the meantime."

"I've heard today that we've just appointed the new store manager. Why don't you contact her and start work on the Design Call together."

The Design Call was an initiative that had started in London. There was a constant stream of designers wanting to pitch their products to Snug, so they had introduced the idea of open calls where anyone who wanted to pitch would be guaranteed a five-minute interview to show their products. It worked amazingly well in helping Snug to source amazing things which were not produced commercially and so would normally be off their radar, and it gave designers the opportunity to be stocked on the high street; normally a very expensive and time-consuming business.

It was considered by the company to be critical to the success of the new store to stock Icelandic designers who were as yet undiscovered. It was going to be a harder job than it was in the UK because the word needed to be spread about the Design Call and as a company, they had no existing links in the country at all. Normally it wouldn't be in Rachel's remit to take on the search for products but this was a special case. Luisa had spearheaded the initial searches in Oslo and Stockholm and it had worked well. And now that the new manager was going to be at a loose end as well, it seemed like the perfect way to fill the extra couple of weeks.

Rachel strolled up the road to fetch coffee for herself and Nick. It was finally just about light at 11 am, so instead of going straight to the coffee shop, she took the opportunity to walk around the block. The buildings were so quirky; most of them had coloured corrugated roofs and cladding and were arranged in quite a higgledy-piggledy way. There were quite a few houses amongst them with gardens, which was a strange juxtaposition with being in the middle of a capital city.

A beautifully knitted hat caught her eye in a shop window on the next street along from Laugavegur. It made her think of Jonas again because it was very similar to the one he'd been wearing and would match her new gloves nicely. She thought how funny it was that she had begun to associate Jonas with knitwear.

Some steps led down into the little nook of a shop which was crammed to the rafters with balls of wool of every shade you could imagine. She scanned around quickly to see where the hats were but couldn't see that there were any, just the one in the window.

"Hi, I was hoping to buy a hat like the one in the window?" she asked shyly, anxious in assuming the woman would understand English, but she needn't have worried, she spoke excellent English, just like every other Icelander Rachel had met so far.

"Ah," she smiled, "you have to knit the hat yourself."

"Oh. Well, thanks anyway."

As she turned to leave the lady asked, "Can you knit?"

"I learnt when I was a child but I've never made anything."

"You should try, it is very easy to knit a hat like that. Why don't you come back this evening or tomorrow and I can help you start?"

Good grief, Rachel thought, she wanted to have the hat now, not in a year or two's time.

"Okay, thanks, I will if I have chance."

Grabbing the coffees on the way back to the shop, she wondered whether Jonas had knitted his hat.

10

That evening, after eating at a delicious pizza restaurant just down the road from the shop, Rachel went back to her room, made a cup of tea and snuggled down into bed. She still hadn't spoken to Adam because he hadn't rung her back the night before as he had said he would and by the time she went to bed, she'd been too tired to care. He knew she'd arrived safely so it didn't really matter.

But now, curious about where he had been the day before, she rang him again.

"Hi, Rach! How's it going?" Adam said cheerfully, "Is it freezing cold?"

"Yes, absolutely bitter. I've already bought some gloves and I tried to buy a hat but it turns out I have to knit my own," she said, rolling her eyes at the memory of it.

"You can't knit, can you?"

"No. Well, I did when I was little. Anyway, what have you been up to?"

"Oh, you know, same as usual. I miss you."

"I miss you too. Today's been a nightmare. The schedule is already over by two weeks because of a problem with the floor."

"God, you've only just got there! Is it still okay for me to come over the weekend after next? I could cancel if things are going badly."

Did he sound like he wanted to cancel?

"It'll be alright by then, Adam, I really want you to come. It's so beautiful, not that I've seen much of it yet, but I went to the Blue

47

Lagoon and honestly, you'd have loved it." He'd have hated it. He had an aversion to swimming pools. "Well, you wouldn't have but it was amazing. Maybe we should go on an excursion or something when you come? Apparently, that's the touristy thing to do," she said, remembering her conversation with Jonas. "Anyway, how's work going with the Scramble thing?"

"Not too bad. Hopefully, it'll all be tied up by the time I come to visit, but you know what it's like, as soon as this deal's finalised, the next one will be full-on."

Adam was right, there was never any let-up. That's what got her down sometimes because he would work crazy hours to get a project finished and you would think there would be some respite from it and then it started again straight away with the next one. She just hoped he could manage one weekend where he wasn't working at full pelt.

"Sorry we didn't get to speak yesterday. Where were you, it sounded so loud." Rachel tried to sound nonchalant, although she was wondering why he hadn't mentioned it already, especially as he hadn't called her back.

"Oh, I met up with Jim for a drink. We went to that bar on Fisherman's Walk. You know the one we went to for Carrie's leaving do." Well, that sounded entirely reasonable. "It was great actually, it's ages since we've done that." He paused as if he was considering what he'd just said.

"Well, I'm glad to hear you're not pining for me too much."

He laughed and she could imagine his smiling face which warmed her heart.

"So, have you managed to see much of Reykjavik yet?"

"I've walked around the block, I know where I can get coffee and I know where the shop is, that's about all so far. I think I might try and find a swimming pool, I won't survive very long without a swim, especially if everything keeps going pear-shaped." She made a mental note to ask at reception about a pool.

"I'm sure things will sort themselves out. It probably just feels worse because you're away and it's all down to you."

"Thanks, Adam. That makes me feel better," she laughed.

"You know what I mean, Rach. You'd be taking this kind of thing in your stride normally."

His words immediately boosted her confidence. He was right, she did relish this kind of challenge at work; it's what made it interesting.

"I know, it just seems different, being here without the team. I'll feel better as soon as I get the flooring sorted out."

"Well, on that note, I will leave you to ponder your schedule. I'll ring you at the weekend. Do you think you'll be working through?"

"I wouldn't think so, there's not much to do yet. I'm going to try and meet up with the new store manager though, so it depends on how that goes."

She wanted the call to last longer, to be able to pretend they were just at home, chatting together about their day.

"It'll be great, Rach. You'll smash it," he said with a smile she could hear in his voice.

"Thanks. Love you, Adam."

"Love you too, Rach. Bye," he said softly, hanging up before she felt ready.

She lay back on the pillows resting the phone on her chest, feeling homesick, not really for home, but to be with Adam. She let herself wallow for a couple of minutes, then considered that even if she was at home they would most likely not be doing anything out of the ordinary. They probably wouldn't be spending the evening gazing into each other's eyes over dinner. She'd most likely be eating alone, wondering what time Adam would get in. That made her smile and snapped her out of her rose-tinted homesick daydream.

In the morning, she decided to venture on a longer walk around the harbour where she hadn't explored yet. She wanted to see the Harpa close up and walk along the seafront because so far she'd only glimpsed it from the roof windows in her hotel room. She was waiting for Gudrun, the new store manager, to return her call having left a message for her the day before about meeting up. With no work to get on with, Nick had flown back to London so there wasn't much else she could do for now.

From the hotel, she walked downhill towards the sea and crossed the road so she could walk next to the low sea wall. Across the bay were huge jagged snow-covered mountains which seemed so unlikely a sight this close to the city but they tempted her into wanting to explore the spectacular scenery.

There was a very brisk wind blowing at the seafront, as it was a flat open area and a wide road away from the closely packed buildings of the town which provided, she realised as the cold crept its way through every part of her, a haven from the wind.

In the dusk of the morning, the window lights of the Harpa were still visible but they were static now unlike the amazing, colour changing spectacle she had seen the day she arrived.

The wind was quite fierce so Rachel was grateful for the warmth that hit her as soon as she walked into the building. The foyer was majestic with a wide but shallow staircase that reached up to the very top floor in one never-ending sweep, with numerous landings to pause at on the way up, to enjoy the space and the view towards the town. On the ground floor in front of her, small corridors led the way through the heart of the building with promises of sea views on the other side. Again, the building opened up at the back and full-height windows were giving an amazing view of the sea and sky, making her feel like she was on a boat right over the water. There were plenty of places to sit and enjoy the peace and quiet so she went back to the foyer and bought a coffee, planning to do just that.

"Hello again."

Rachel looked around and saw Jonas standing there with an armful of leaflets.

"Oh, hi!"

It was funny seeing someone from here who knew her.

"How are you enjoying Reykjavik so far?" He smiled at her, his eyes wrinkling at the corners, looking like he was really pleased to see her.

"Well, this is the first place I've been to apart from the hotel and the shop but yes, I love it, it's beautiful. I can't wait to see more of it."

He nodded his head towards his mountain of leaflets.

"Take one of these, I am just delivering them around town, it's our latest brochure."

Rachel slid one off the top of his pile. "My boyfriend is coming to visit in a couple of weeks so I might book something. I'll let you know, thanks."

Mentioning Adam to Jonas felt odd, for some reason, and left her feeling flustered, so she busily tended to her coffee while she thought of something else to say.

"Do you know a swimming pool here that's within walking

distance?"

"There is a great pool called Laugardalslaug, it's a twenty-minute walk but you could get the number fourteen bus which stops right outside."

"I don't think I'm brave enough to try catching a bus just yet." she laughed.

"I am going there today to deliver leaflets, why don't you come so you know how to find it?"

"Oh no, gosh, don't worry, I'm happy to walk."

"No, I am going there anyway. What are you doing now?" He was already making as if to leave, full of enthusiasm, eyes wide, clearly keen for her to go with him.

"Nothing really... okay then, thanks, Jonas. Let me at least buy you a coffee to take as well."

It was hard to judge walking distances when you were in a car, but Jonas's estimate of twenty minutes seemed plausible and Rachel was pretty sure she would remember how to find it again. Jonas dropped his leaflets off and had a brief chat with the girl at the reception desk.

"We can have a look round if you like?" he said.

They went through a door to the left of the desk, outdoors, onto the poolside which was surrounded by squashy tarmac like you find in children's playgrounds. There was an Olympic-sized swimming pool, a leisure pool and slide and yet another pool nearest to the door which was steaming with heat and had ledges to sit on; more like a network of deep streams than a pool. This by far had the most people in it, everyone was sitting and chatting.

"Coming here to the pool is a social thing in Iceland, a bit like going to the pub in England," explained Jonas. "Everyone meets here and sits in the hot pots talking."

He gestured over towards four sets of railings circling hot tubs which you stepped down and into via a spiral staircase. They each had a sign hung on the outside stating the temperatures, ranging from 36°C to 42°C.

"I think those would be too hot for me," said Rachel, smiling.

"You would get used to it, gradually build up to the hottest," he grinned. "Hey, come over here." He took her hand led her towards the other end of the pool area. "This is the saltwater pool. They pump the seawater from the bay and it is warmed naturally by the geothermal activity. All the water here is heated like that."

All she could think about as he talked was that they were holding hands. Was that okay? It seemed like second nature to Jonas but it was giving Rachel butterflies. After the brief kiss he had given her when he'd dropped her off at the hotel and now this...perhaps he was just a tactile person, Rachel thought.

"It looks so inviting, I'm definitely trying this," she said, taking her hand from his and dipping it into the water. "It is so lovely and warm!"

"Yes, it's my favourite of all the pools here. Very relaxing."

As they wandered back towards the main building, she snuck a glance at him and he caught her eye and smiled.

"Thanks for bringing me here, it's cool."

"It was a pleasure," he said, looking right into her eyes as if trying to convey something else. "It's fun to show you around."

His ready smile faded slightly and he looked so sincerely at her that she found herself looking back into his eyes, completely mesmerised.

"Look, I'm going to walk back just so I know how long it takes," Rachel said brightly, trying to break the moment that Jonas had created between them. It wasn't awkward but it was something.

"Okay." He leaned over and kissed her on the cheek just as he had before when he'd left her at the hotel. "Bye, Rachel, I hope I see you again soon."

She watched him walk towards his jeep, then he stopped and turned around.

"Could I take you out for something to eat tonight?" he called, shrugging his shoulders and giving her a lopsided smile.

"What did you have in mind?" She would be ready to nip it in the bud if it sounded anything like a date but on the other hand, she wasn't about to turn down the offer of eating dinner with somebody rather than being alone.

"Have you been to the Noodle Bar yet?" Now he was grinning and walking slowly back towards her. "It's famous for its noodle soup."

"That sounds good, I haven't been anywhere to eat properly yet."

"I'll meet you at 7 pm at your hotel, does that sound okay?"

"Perfect. I'll see you later."

He turned back towards his jeep leaving Rachel with a big smile on her face, wondering whether she was crazy to be going out with him. It could end in trouble. But she had told him about Adam and he might have a partner himself, she didn't know. It wasn't as if he had explicitly said that it was a date. He was probably just being friendly because he knew she was by herself and his job was showing people around. Or was she kidding herself because she couldn't deny that she felt great when she was with Jonas and she wanted to see him again.

As she walked back to town under a constantly changing sky, Rachel tried to justify her decision to go out with Jonas. It was entirely possible for men and women to be friends and there was no evidence, apart from a slight flutter in her stomach, to suggest that there was anything more than that between them. She could easily put him in the 'friend' category. The feelings she was having were probably because they had just met; an initial attraction which would wear off to be a friendship. Definitely fine.

She got to the shop and as she wrestled with the slightly sticky front door, the flooring company phoned to inform her that they could start the job in two weeks. It could have been worse and all she could do now was concentrate on organising the Design Call with the new manager and try to keep herself from being distracted by anything else.

11

Rachel waited in the hotel foyer glancing up every time the door opened, wondering whether all men were tardy or just the ones that were meeting her.

She'd just rung Anna to tell her about the dinner date with Jonas. It seemed less clandestine if someone else knew.

"Rachel, there is nothing wrong with having a friendship with a man," she'd said, "or going out for dinner with a man. Just because he's good looking and you probably fancy him, it doesn't mean you're being unfaithful to Adam."

Wise words. Rachel had told her he was good looking. He was, it was just a fact, not even an opinion. And he was the only person she knew here.

Perhaps she should have waited outside, she wondered, at which point Jonas came bursting through the door.

"Sorry, Rachel, I came straight from the office. I had to cancel tonight's Northern Lights excursion and it took longer than I thought."

"Why did you have to cancel it?"

"The aurora forecast is not good for tonight, we would be unlikely to see the lights so we cancelled but people who had a booking can go the next time instead. Tomorrow we will try again."

"Oh, so they just stay on the list until the chances are good?"

"Exactly," he said, taking her hand and leading them up the road towards Laugavegur.

The Noodle Bar was not somewhere Rachel would have chosen

to eat in a million years. It was very small and looked a bit on the grubby side. Not wanting to offend Jonas, she could only hope that Icelandic health and safety inspections were as rigorous as they seemed to be at home. She was sure they were; Scandinavians seemed very fastidious in general. The windows were steamed up so you couldn't really see inside and all it had was 'Noodle Bar' sign-written on the window in red paint. Rachel gave Jonas a dubious look as they stood outside.

"I know it doesn't look good but the food is fantastic, it is an experience you have to have while you are here," he insisted. "Shall I order for us? There is beef, chicken or vegetable."

"Beef, chicken or vegetable what?" said Rachel, needing some clarification on what she was ordering.

"The noodles and broth are all the same but you can have them with beef, chicken or vegetables. Then you can have other things on top like crispy onions if you want to, and fish sauce."

"Oh, okay, well vegetable then please."

No way was she going to risk the meat, just in case. She didn't think she had ever been anywhere to eat that had just one thing on the menu and she wasn't sure if that was a good sign or a bad one. They ladled a pile of noodles into each bowl then covered them in broth and vegetables, adding Jonas's meat after that. Then they chose extra garnishes; crispy onions for Rachel and everything for Jonas as far as she could tell; fish sauce, extra chillies, unidentifiable items.

There weren't any normal tables, just high bar tables with stools around the edge of the small shop. It could probably only seat about eight people at a time but as it was the definition of fast food, they probably wouldn't be there very long anyway.

It just goes to show that you shouldn't judge things on their looks; the noodles were the best dish of any Asian origin that Rachel had ever tasted. She couldn't begin to explain how delicious they were, but part of the appeal was that they warmed you from within without being very spicy to eat. In a frozen country, that was a definite advantage. She knew it wouldn't be the last time she visited the Noodle Bar. Apart from anything else it was the perfect place to eat if you were alone.

Back out in the bracing night air, Rachel conceded to Jonas, "Honestly, I never would have chosen to eat there but it was amazing, absolutely delicious! Thanks for taking me."

She pushed her hands deep into her pockets. They had only been in there about fifteen minutes and she wondered whether to announce that she was going to go back to the hotel or whether that was a bit rude given that it was Jonas's invitation, so she waited to see what he was going to suggest next.

"Shall we go for a quick drink? It's still early," he suggested, smiling but shrugging his shoulders as seemed to be his habit as if it didn't matter to him either way.

Rachel nodded and they set off down the hill, not too far, to a small, virtually empty bar. It offered speciality beers from all over the world, listed on a huge blackboard. Rachel didn't know where to start so she told Jonas that she'd have whatever he was having. Furnished with two bottles of Icelandic beer, they sat in the window at a small table that had a little tea light to soften the darkness.

The candlelight cast a romantic hue over them both and Rachel couldn't seem to look at Jonas without noticing how gorgeous he was while at the same time trying to stop herself from thinking about him in that way. To try and distract herself and get back to real life where Adam was the person she should find the most attractive, she asked Jonas if he had a partner.

"No, not at the moment. I had a girlfriend, Hilde, for four years but she got a job in the US. We tried to carry on, visited each other every few weeks but it didn't work. If it had been short term it would have been fine but she wanted to stay over there and she wanted me to go too but I have my business here, I don't know what I would do anywhere else. So, we split up about six months ago." He fiddled with his beer bottle as he spoke, not meeting her eye and when he did look at her, he looked sad.

"Four years is a long time, it must have been really hard."

"It was difficult but it wasn't fair on either of us to make the other compromise so much to be together. We wouldn't have been happy in the end if we had. So yes, it was sad but it was the best thing to do."

Jonas sounded pragmatic, perhaps only with the benefit of hindsight, but it made Rachel think that maybe she and Adam were in danger of forcing compromise onto each other and that perhaps their relationship could be in jeopardy if they did. Jonas and Hilde were living on different continents which made it more difficult to do anything except decide to move your world to be together and that was a big ask of anyone. At least she and Adam were usually living in the same place.

"How about you, how long have you been with your boyfriend?"

"About two years. We live together in London and we're planning to get married at some point."

Jonas raised his eyebrows in question.

"I mean, he hasn't proposed but that's the plan."

It sounded ridiculous as she explained. Ridiculous that she needed to explain in the first place and it suddenly struck her that it wasn't very romantic. If Adam ever proposed it wasn't exactly going to be a surprise.

"Did he mind you coming to Iceland?"

"No, not really, it was for work, kind of a promotion, so I wanted to come. The thing is, it was meant to be just for three weeks but we had a problem with the flooring in the shop and now it'll be more like five weeks in the end. But he's coming to visit next weekend so that'll be nice."

She felt as though she was trying to justify her relationship with Adam but it was almost to herself more than to Jonas.

"You must miss him." Jonas looked at her sincerely, his eyes catching the flicker of the candle.

"I do." The beer had made her less guarded. "But I was looking forward to some time apart just so that we would have the chance to miss each other and be more appreciative of each other maybe?"

"Hmm, Hilde thought the same. She thought being away would make us realise what we had together instead of taking it for granted. It worked, I missed her but she moved on to a whole new life and I couldn't be part of it."

"Well, at least I'll be going back to London, that's a good start." Rachel joked, trying to lighten the mood.

"Yes, it is," Jonas smiled. "Let's drink to that. Skál!" He tapped his bottle against hers. "I am empty. Do you want another?"

"This one's on me," she said, getting up. "Do you want the same again?"

The second beer was their last, then Jonas walked her back to the hotel along the seafront, past the Harpa which was lit up again in its shimmering greens and purples. She enjoyed his company, he was funny and charming in a very down to earth way. Not trying to

57

impress her, just being friendly. Spending the evening with him and hearing him talk so frankly about his relationship had made Rachel wonder what being apart from Adam would do to theirs in the end. Would absence make their hearts grow fonder as she had hoped or had she put herself in the position of being out of sight, out of mind? She couldn't help but think maybe she was like Hilde and had been open to the idea of being apart for a while, hoping to strengthen things while she left someone behind who wasn't into the idea at all.

12

With the shop fit on hold, Rachel decided that she could afford to have a lazy Sunday. She woke up about 9 am and ordered breakfast in bed with two pots of tea so that she could have cup-after-cup. She propped her MacBook on the bed next to her and started to watch back-to-back episodes of Friends. Bliss.

Her phone rang. It was her mother. Taking a deep breath, she answered, with half an eye still on her New York buddies.

"Hi, Mum."

"Hello, Rachel! How are you, love? What time is it in Iceland?"

"Um, I don't know, I think it's the same time as it is there?"

"Well, it's quarter past ten here. Anyway, I was talking to Cynthia at WI and she said that there is a wonderful wool shop in Reykjavik." Here we go...

"Yep, I popped in there, I know where that is. Do you want me to get you something?"

"What were you doing in there? You haven't started knitting have you?" she said incredulously.

"It was just an accident, I - " but her mother was in full flow and she cut Rachel off before she had the chance to explain her apparently strange behaviour.

"I don't want you to go to any trouble but Cynthia and I were looking at an Icelandic sweater pattern on the web and I've got a list of what we both want. The Icelandic wool is very good value, Rachel."

"Oh, okay, yes that's fine. Can you email your list to me?"

"I'll get Dad to do it for me. Now, when you go into the shop, can you have a look at the pinks because there is a rose pink and a dusky pink and it's very hard to tell exactly what they look like on the web. I want the one which goes the best with the cloud blue, so I'll leave it to you to decide, love." Brilliant, as if she would have any clue.

"Alright Mum, I'll go and see if it's open later if you get Dad to send the list. Do you want me to post it or can you wait for me to bring it home?"

"It'll cost a fortune to post! We're not in any rush, Rachel, just pack it in your case." Hmm, two jumpers' worth of wool would probably fill her case but she could always give it to Adam to take back. She suggested that to her mum.

"Oh, Adam's coming to visit, is he?" She couldn't have sounded more disbelieving. "Can he manage to get the time off?"

"Yes, Mum. He's coming next weekend. I'll get him to post it when he gets back."

"Don't put him to any trouble, Rachel, I know how busy he is," she said, in the uptight, disapproving voice that she saved especially for Adam.

"He won't mind, Mum."

He would mind but Rachel would just force him to do it. It would win him some brownie points with her mum at least.

It turned out that there were only so many episodes of Friends that she could manage to watch in one go and by midday, when her phone pinged with the email from her dad, she'd had enough of festering in bed so she ventured out on a wool run.

She didn't know whether any of the shops would be open on a Sunday but almost everything was, including the little wool shop on Skólavörðustígur.

Her mum's email was a list of numbers, names and quantities and when she picked up a random ball of wool to see if she could make out the system, she didn't know where to start. She must have looked like she was out of her depth, studying her phone and the ball of wool in a state of confusion because the lady from the other day when she had called in about the hats asked her if she needed any help. Rachel explained about the list from her mum and she didn't seem to think it was odd at all, just took the phone and started pulling out balls of wool and making a pile of them on the counter.

Even a rookie wool chooser like Rachel could see that the pink on the list was too bright so she swapped it for a different, softer pink.

Slightly doubting her maths, Rachel tried to work out how much it was going to cost and thought it worked out at about £1.50 a ball. Having once bought yarn from John Lewis, with plenty of input from the sales assistant, for her mum to knit her a jumper, she knew that that was pretty cheap. No wonder her mum and Cynthia were so keen.

She wandered over to the window display and counted the colours in the hat. There were six which meant it would cost less than ten pounds to knit. How much it would cost in stress and frustration was another matter but she was tempted to have a go; at least it would give her something to do in the evenings.

"Is that hat really easy to knit?" she asked, doubtfully.

"Yes, the pattern is a chart, a bit like a picture of the stitches so you just follow that. I can show you how to start now if you would like?"

"Thanks, that would be great." Ooh, she was quite excited now and could always watch some YouTube knitting videos if she got stuck.

"Do you like those colours or do you want to choose something else?" the knitting lady asked, pulling out a pair of knitting needles from a large pot of all different sizes.

"Yes, exactly like that one is perfect." It probably wouldn't look the same as that in the end, thought Rachel assuming her knitting skills were not quite up to that standard but it would be fun to try. Her mum would think it was great even if no-one else did.

Half an hour later Rachel was furnished with wool (a lot of wool but at least it was lightweight), needles, a pattern and a vague idea of what she was doing. She picked up a latte from Te & Kaffi around the corner and began to wander back to the hotel to start her knitting.

The sky had darkened since she'd left the hotel earlier and it seemed like dusk although it wasn't late enough yet. As she strolled, looking over the sea towards the mountains, it began to snow, very heavily, reducing the visibility completely so that the only things she could make out were the very nearest buildings. Struggling with her bulky bags and trying not to drop her coffee, she pulled her hood up over her hat in a vain attempt to try and keep the driving snow out of her face. The snow was settling with surprising speed; the coloured roofs had already disappeared and the roads were covered in a perfect blanket of white with hardly any cars to spoil it. Despite the battle it was becoming to put one foot in front of the other, it was quite exciting. They hardly ever had snow in London so it was a few years since Rachel had seen any and she loved being the first to walk on the untouched powder that was paving the way in front of her.

She had made it onto Laugavegur and knew that the shop was just ahead. The thought of being able to take shelter now without having to haul her massive bags any further was overwhelming. She dug the keys out of her bag and let herself in, kicking the door shut firmly behind her.

Stamping her feet to get the worst of the snow off and shaking it off her coat before it could soak through, she sighed happily and sat on the floor sipping her lukewarm coffee watching the snow fall quietly outside. The fairy lights in the trees made it a perfect winter picture, one which she wanted to show someone. She pulled her phone out and Facetimed Adam. It took him a minute to answer by which time Rachel had positioned herself with her back to the window so that he could see the snow.

"Hey Rach," he said in a sleepy voice.

"Look it's snowing!"

"Oh, great. All I can see is a black you in front of a bright light." He sounded less than enthusiastic but Rachel was undeterred.

"Wait a sec and I'll take you outside." She pulled her coat on again and went to open the door but it was latched. She put down the phone, all the while imagining Adam rolling his eyes in exasperation and flicked the door lock. Nothing.

"Shit. I can't open the door." She flicked the lock again and shook the door handle but it still didn't open.

"Well don't worry. Show me the next time it snows."

"But I can't get out! The door's stuck or jammed or something." Rachel picked the phone up again to see Adam looking remarkably calm given her plight.

"Can't you ring someone to come and help you?"

"It's Sunday, there's a snowstorm and besides that, I don't know anyone!"

"Alright, don't panic. Show me the door." She scanned her phone across the lock. "Hmm, I don't know. Perhaps it's jammed or something."

"Oh thanks, Einstein. I think I've already established that!"

"Well, what do you expect me to do? You'll have to call someone."

"Great, thanks so much for your help."

"No problem," said Adam, her sarcasm completely passing him by. "Good luck, Rach. Let me know how you get on."

Rachel sat for a moment contemplating her options. She could call a locksmith. It would cost a small fortune and she'd look like an idiot with her Snug colleagues when they inevitably found out that she'd managed to lock herself into the shop even though she had the keys. Anyway, maybe it wasn't the lock, Nick had had no problems with it the other day. She could call the hotel to see if they had anyone who could come and help her. Unlikely given that it was a Sunday and when she had left it had looked like there was just one person on duty. Jonas. Could she ask him? They were kind of friends by now. Yes, it would be a bit embarrassing but she was sure he'd be nice about it, whatever the problem and at least he wasn't a complete stranger.

Rachel scrolled through her contacts. She'd been given a mobile number by the tour company for the Blue Lagoon excursion in case she'd needed to contact the tour guide on the day. Obviously, on that day it had been Jonas who had the phone but maybe it wasn't always him who would answer. But, she reasoned, they might be able to give her his personal number if she explained. It was worth a try.

She pressed the number in her contacts and held her breath.

"Iceland Adventures, Jonas speaking." Thank God.

"Hi Jonas, it's Rachel. I hope it was alright to call you on this number?"

"Of course, it's nice to hear from you." He sounded like he meant it.

"Well, I'm in a bit of a pickle. I've locked myself in the shop and I don't know anyone else I can ask to help me. I mean, I don't even know where you live and it's a snowstorm and…"

"Rachel it's alright." He sounded so reassuring that Rachel instantly felt as if everything was going to be fine. "I am five minutes away. Don't worry."

"Thank you so much, Jonas."

She hung up and exhaled. Now that she'd called him and he was coming to the rescue she felt sure that the door would miraculously open just to make her look like a fool but no, when she tried it again it was still firmly stuck. Well, that was something.

Nobody had walked by in the entire time she'd been looking out of the window so when she saw a figure crossing the road, she knew it must be Jonas. He was smiling at her as he approached the door.

"Thank you, Jonas," she called loudly through the door. "I'm so sorry to call you. I just didn't know what to do."

"It's fine. I love being out in the snow."

She could tell by his expression that he meant that.

"Can you pass the keys out to me? Maybe I can let myself in."

Rachel posted them through the letterbox and Jonas caught them and tried to unlock the door. He tried the main lock but that didn't work, then he tried something else which Rachel couldn't see but whatever it had been meant that the main lock worked and he was letting himself in.

"Oh my God! Thank you! Don't let the door close behind you!" Rachel went to grab the door but there was no need as Jonas was holding it slightly open.

"It looks like the *dauðbolti* had partly locked. Did you slam the door? It must be very loose for that to happen.

"The deadbolt? I did kick it shut when I came in. Do you think that was what it was?"

Jonas shrugged. "Probably."

He made sure the bolt was back and gently closed the door. Rachel held her breath. The last thing she needed was for both of them to be locked in but when he tried to open it again, it opened the first time.

"I think you just need to be gentle with it and get it changed sometime. What are you doing here anyway?" he asked, with an amused smile.

"I was just sheltering from the snow. I had my hands full," she gestured to her bags of wool, "which is why I kicked the door."

"You're a big knitter then?"

"Oh God, no. This is for my mum. She sent me a list."

"Right. Well, are you staying here or shall I help you lock up?"

"No, I think I will get going."

Rachel collected the bags and stood aside as Jonas locked the shop door then handed the keys to her. He took one of her bags without saying anything and they headed in the direction of the hotel together.

A good few centimetres of perfect snow-covered the pavements and it gently crunched under their snow boots as they walked in easy silence. The sky was still dark with clouds promising more of the same although the snowfall had slowed to a few floating flakes for now.

As they approached the hotel, Jonas handed the bag of wool back to Rachel and dug his hands into his pockets.

"Well, it was nice to be able to come to your rescue, Rachel."

"Thank you so much, Jonas. Who knows how long I'd have been there."

He smiled and she could feel her heart begin to beat slightly harder as she waited for the inevitable kiss on the cheek.

"Bye Rachel." The briefest kiss touched her cheek and then he turned and walked away, disappearing into the gently falling snow and ever fading light.

"Bye Jonas," she whispered to herself.

After a hot bubbly bath and with a glass of wine, purely for Dutch courage as she entered the unknown realms of knitting, Rachel sat on the bed trying to knit.

Over an hour, and several rows of slightly uneven but nevertheless pleasing knitting later, her phone rang. It was Adam.

"Hey, Rach. How's it going? You obviously managed to get out of the shop in the end?" She put her knitting down and hugged her knees to her chest.

"Yes, no thanks to you." She shouldn't be cross with him. What could he have done to help? Nevertheless, he could have tried sounding supportive.

"I'm really sorry, Rach. I was asleep when you called so I wasn't really with it."

He was asleep in the middle of the day? That was pretty much unheard of even on a Sunday.

"It's okay. I called a guy from the tour company I used for the Blue Lagoon. We've bumped into each other a couple of times so, you know, he's the only person I know here."

"Right...well, at least you had someone to call. So, what are you up to now?"

"I'm just having a glass of wine and doing some knitting," she said defensively.

"Oh my God, you're knitting that hat? Things must be bad." he joked.

"Very funny. Actually, I'm quite enjoying it and you'll be really impressed when you see it."

"As long as you don't knit one for me."

"You don't even know what it looks like!" she said, feigning outrage. "You'll be begging me to knit one for you."

"Oh really," he said, drily.

"Did you go out last night?"

"Yes, I went out with Jim, it was great. We went to that club in Soho that you went to with Anna the other week. I felt a bit rough earlier but we went out for a full English and a hair-of-the-dog, so now I just feel tired." So that was why he was asleep. "Anyway, I was ringing to let you know that I've booked a flight for the weekend after next. Is that going to be alright because if not I've got a flex ticket so I can always change it?"

"No, that's perfect," Rachel said, trying to put the niggling question of how Adam had managed to fit in two nights out with Jim since she'd been away, out of her mind, "I should be able to have the weekend off because they'll only just have finished the floor. It's great timing."

"Fantastic. I'll email you the flight details but I'm arriving Friday night and leaving Sunday night. Does that sound okay?"

"Yes, fine. Do you want me to come and meet you?"

"No, don't worry, I've organised a car to pick me up so I'll come straight to the hotel."   Rachel was pretty sure his PA had done all this organising for him which was the only reason it had happened.

"I'm going to book some things for us to do that I've been saving until you come."

"Great, as long as it's not swimming."

It was ages since they had spent a whole uninterrupted weekend together so she was going to make it special. After all, when they saw each other again, she was hoping for sparks galore. The fact that she didn't feel like that now was just a blip.

After they finished talking, Rachel rummaged in her bag to find the brochure that Jonas had given her. It had a brief description of what she now knew was the obligatory Golden Circle tour, they would definitely do that one. Could they fit in a Northern Lights excursion too? It would be amazing to see them here together. She flicked through looking at the more adventurous things on offer. Two weeks before she had to properly start work and Luisa *had* told her to relax. Even organising the Design Call wasn't going to take all that time…

13

On Monday morning Rachel went to the shop to meet the new manager, Gudrun. Having spoken briefly on the phone, they had arranged to meet so that Rachel could go through the plans with her. The locations and floor space that would be allocated to the visual merchandising all needed deciding as well as the positions for the mock-up rooms and all the little things that weren't on the main drawings of the internal build. It was a great opportunity for Gudrun to be involved right at the beginning which could only be good for the store.

At 9 am there was a knock and Rachel opened the door to find Gudrun on the doorstep, grinning.

"Hello, you must be Rachel! It is great to meet you," she said, enthusiastically holding out her hand to shake.

"Great to meet you too, Gudrun. Come in!"

They shook hands as she walked through the door, her face full of wonder in the manner of a kid seeing Disneyland for the first time.

"Wow, it's an amazing space!"

"It is indeed," Rachel agreed. "Have you been in here before?"

"Yes, it used to be a clothes shop. A bit too old-fashioned for me but my mother loved it. It looks so different now it's empty."

They chatted easily about where Gudrun had worked before and what experience she had which she felt would be good for Snug. Gudrun had moved to Norway after university and had worked her way up in one of the big department stores until she had met her partner and they'd decided to move back to Iceland. Rachel knew they were lucky to have found someone with such a breadth of experience who was happy to manage just one store at this stage in their career but Gudrun seemed content and brushed aside Rachel's observation saying that there were more important things than work.

"So," said Rachel, standing up, "let's start by walking around and we'll just have a chat about how a Snug store would normally be laid out."

As they did so, Rachel answered Gudrun's questions and listened to her ideas about the placement of various things, some of which were different to other Snug stores but Rachel was impressed; Gudrun clearly had a flair for this kind of thing.

Halfway through the morning, Gudrun popped to the coffee shop and when she got back they sat cross-legged on the floor, which was in the middle of being gradually repaired, and got to know each other a little better.

"How are you finding Iceland?" she asked Rachel.

"I love it, what I've seen anyway. I'm just about to book a Golden Circle tour for the weekend after next. My boyfriend's coming to visit."

"Ah, yes. We did that tour for a school trip when I was little. And if we ever have visitors we take them on that. It's really good for seeing lots of the best things in one go."

"That's what I've heard. I really fancy going to a natural hot pool as well."

"There's a really good one not far outside Reykjavik. I could take you sometime if you like."

"Brilliant, thanks. So, what made you move back from Norway?"

"I grew up here and then left the minute I could. I couldn't wait to leave but maybe that's what made me realise how much I loved it. Lots of people go away to university but most come back. I loved working in Norway but it was an easy decision to make when Olafur wanted to move back to work here."

"Well, it's great that you both wanted to do that," Rachel smiled.

"He was worth the move back. He works for a tour company, Iceland Adventures."

"Oh," said Rachel rummaging in her bag, "that's the one I have the leaflet for. The one that Jonas owns?"

"Yes! Have you met him? He's such a great guy. It's the best tour company in the country and I'm not just saying that because Olafur works for him."

"Olafur and Jonas picked me up from the airport and I've bumped into Jonas a couple of times since then. He rescued me when I got locked in here yesterday."

Gudrun's eyebrows disappeared into her hair.

"Anyway, he does seem really nice."

"He works too hard. Well, since his girlfriend left anyway, but that's how he's made such a success of it, I suppose."

Once Gudrun had left, Rachel rang Jonas's company and booked a glacier walking trip for herself as she had a couple of free days coming up. It seemed like an adventurous yet relatively safe choice and she was determined to see as much of the country as she could.

Having had such a productive day, she decided to go to Laugardalslaug for a swim and now, she was feeling brave enough to go on the bus. She knew she needed a number 14, she knew where she was going and she knew where to catch the bus. Sorted. After locking up the shop and then ducking into the hotel to collect her swimming kit, she was off.

After doing her requisite thirty lengths in the main pool, she treated herself to a long leisurely soak in the salt pool. Even after she had encountered it at the Blue Lagoon, it had been somewhat of a culture shock coming here and finding out that you had to thoroughly shower completely starkers before you put your cossie on and got in the pool. And at this pool, there was an attendant in the changing room to check that everyone did. The only good thing Rachel could say about it was that no-one gave it a second thought, it was just the way things were done so despite it going against every grain in her prudish British body, she didn't feel too bad about it in the end.

It was complete bliss being in the hot thermal water while it was freezing cold outside. The sky was clear and the lights not so bright that you couldn't see the stars. She lay there hoping for a glimpse of the Northern Lights. Well, half-hoping because it would be so romantic if the first time she saw them she was with Adam. Or Jonas. No, not Jonas. Rachel tried to stop thinking about him but he popped into her head all the more easily, even when she tried to concentrate on Adam. So she allowed herself a little moment of fantasy. After all, what was the harm in that?

On her way home, she sampled the joys of an Icelandic hot dog from the kiosk outside the swimming pool which, according to Jonas, was famous along the same lines as the Noodle Bar. On the face of it, it was a normal American style hot dog in a bun but it was served with crispy onions, ketchup, mustard and some mysterious sauce which made it taste completely amazing. It was exactly the right kind of food for after a swim with the only downside being that there was nowhere to sit, just a canopy to stand under so at least you didn't get covered by a layer of snow while you ate.

Since the snowstorm on Sunday, it had snowed most days and because it was so cold it never had a chance to melt. The pavements around the pool, which was outside of the centre of town, had been sprinkled with black grit which Rachel assumed must be ground up lava as there would be a plentiful supply of that, but it had no effect on melting the snow like the grit did at home, it just served to give you a better grip. There was easily fifteen centimetres of icy compacted snow everywhere apart from the pavements right in the middle of town and she was glad she had bought snow boots with her because they were an absolute necessity.

Rachel was just finishing her hot dog when the bus pulled up on the opposite side of the road. Not wanting to have to wait for the next one she ran towards it waving her arms to attract the driver's attention, not that she was sure how much good that would do because it wouldn't work in London, that was for sure. But Reykjavik, as she had already discovered, was nothing like London and he did wait for her. She gazed out of the window at the houses as the bus ambled past and she wondered who lived in them. This was the capital city of the country and yet it didn't feel like that. It wasn't anonymous and full of its own importance. It was friendly and wore its heart on its sleeve. She was falling in love with it.

14

The morning of Rachel's glacier walking excursion arrived and when the jeep pulled up outside the hotel, she was surprised how pleased she was to find that Jonas was the guide.

"Good morning, Rachel! I saw that you were on the list for today. You'll love it," he said, as he held the door of the jeep open for her.

There were already four other people in the back and they all greeted her as she climbed into the front seat. Was it a coincidence, she wondered, that Jonas had picked her up last knowing that then she'd have to sit in the front with him? Also, she couldn't help wondering in a moment of self-indulgent daydreaming (which made her smile inside) whether he always hosted this trip or had he chosen to because she was on the list? Then she silently berated herself for thinking such a ridiculous thing. As if he would go to all that trouble.

"We are going to drive about ninety minutes to the Sólheimajökull glacier," Jonas announced to them all as he pulled away and headed out of the city. "It is good weather for glacier walking today, cold and bright!"

Everyone chuckled appreciatively and Jonas turned and grinned at Rachel, clearly looking forward to the day as much as the rest of them.

"Don't you get bored going to the same places all the time?" she asked.

"No, not at all. Every time you go you see something different. In the summer the ground is covered with flowers and heathers, not that you would believe that when you see it like this," he said, gesturing to the endless white landscape, "but even today the glacier will be different to the last time I saw it. The waterfalls will be flowing more than last time, or less maybe, it has been so cold. There is always something to see."

The exuberance which had been there just a minute ago had vanished and instead there was a gentle but sincere passion as Jonas spoke. He had stopped smiling and when he glanced sideways at Rachel her heart melted at the tenderness in his eyes and if she didn't know better, she'd say a rush of love swept over her at that moment.

"I love that you take the time to notice everything even though you've seen it a hundred times before. You never get tired of the wonder. That's what life's all about, isn't it? And everyone just forgets until they come somewhere like this and then it's wonderful and you feel like you've been walking around your whole life with your eyes closed."

Jonas nodded but kept his eyes on the road. Rachel gazed out of the window trying to memorise every inch of what she saw. At first glance, it was just a snow-covered landscape but there were tiny details which made it spectacular. The wind dusting the snow from the tops of the mountains into the brightest blue sky and a column of steam rising from the snow where a hot spring had punched through every so often were a couple of images Rachel was never going to forget. Iceland was starting to open her eyes to all sorts of things to the point where she felt like she was drifting away from her real life. But she didn't mind that, at the moment. Let it happen while it could, while she was enjoying herself. Real life would be back again soon enough.

"You can see the glacier up ahead," Jonas explained as they arrived. "You can see the edge of it where the rock meets the ice. We'll hike up to the edge and then put crampons on to walk on the ice."

He pulled the jeep into a large clearing and everyone piled out, collecting ice axes and crampons out of the back before they set off across the lava field towards the ice. The other people on the tour were couples so Rachel naturally found herself walking with Jonas at the front of the party.

"Do you do much hiking, Rachel?"

"No, not really," she said, trying to make her breathing sound normal and less like someone who smoked twenty a day. "There's nowhere to hike near where I live."

It struck her as funny that on holiday she was perfectly willing to travel an hour and a half to hike a glacier in a day but at home that would be out of the question. Aside from there being no glaciers in London, she would never travel for ninety minutes to find a hill to walk up.

"It's quite a steep incline. Quite tough if you're not used to hills." Was he smirking slightly?

"Oh, I'm fine. I think it's the cold air more than anything."

"Hey guys," said Jonas, turning around to address the group. "We're just coming up to the ice now so it's a good time to put your crampons on."

He had put his crampons on while Rachel was still turning hers over and over in her hands, working out where to start.

"Here, let me help," he said, bending down and taking her foot, forcing her to hold on to his shoulder for balance.

"Thanks."

"You're welcome." His eyes twinkled as he glanced up to smile at her. "I'm going to go ahead so that I can give everyone a hand up onto the shelf. Will you be okay?"

Rachel nodded with what she hoped was a confident grin, while inside she was wondering whether the crampons were going to be any match for the sheet of ice in front of her.

Falling to the back of the group, Rachel walked unsurely at first until she realised she could trust the crampons, up towards where Jonas was standing on the edge of the glacier. He had bedded himself into the slope, leaning against it next to the path with an ice axe in his left hand anchoring him to the ice and his feet planted firmly so that he could help to haul his guests up onto the glacier.

When it was her turn, Rachel grabbed Jonas's hand and threw herself towards the slope. In the same split second that her feet easily found a grip in the ice, she could feel her hand slip out of her glove and away from Jonas's reassuring grasp. She felt herself fall backwards, in slow motion; she had time to know that she was falling and there was nothing she could do to stop herself aside from reaching in vain towards the slope with the ice axe that was in her other hand. Then she felt a strong hand around her wrist and was immediately steadied.

"Okay, Rachel?" Jonas asked in such a commanding way that it took her breath away as he pulled her up to him with a force that threw her against his body. He was so strong and reassuring in that instant, wrapping his free arm around her shoulders and holding her close until he was sure she was alright.

"Yes, yes, I think I'm fine." She took a deep breath as she took in what had just happened. "Oh my God. That was close."

He helped her up to the glacier before climbing up there himself. Her hand, minus its glove was resting on her chest as if to try and calm her heartbeat after the shock. Jonas put his hands on her shoulders, his eyes searching her face as if trying to assess if she was indeed okay.

"Take a minute, get your breath back. It's all easy walking from here. Are you alright to carry on?"

He rubbed her shoulders briefly before reaching into his rucksack and offering her a flask. It was a warm, slightly spiced milky drink and it relaxed her immediately.

One of the other hikers had retrieved Rachel's glove. She could carry on; it was just a scare and even if she'd fallen it wouldn't have been that far, but she was pretty sure that the ice wouldn't have made for a soft landing. They walked on with Jonas insistently holding her hand which she didn't mind at all. She was still a little shaken.

The scenery was spectacular. It felt as though they were exploring an undiscovered world. After an hour or so of hiking on the glacier, Jonas led them towards the side, near to the foot of a mountain.

"We're going to hike down this trail into a glacial cave," Jonas said, turning to address the group. "Keep to the sides of the path where the ice is less compacted and watch your heads once we get down there."

Still gripping Rachel's hand, which she was now even more grateful for, he led the way down the trail. It wasn't far at all; it was as if they had been in the kitchen and were just nipping down to the cellar. The word 'cave' had led Rachel to assume a dark, wet, grey cave and it couldn't have been more different to that. It was an ice blue, bright space underneath the glacier. The sunlight streamed in, through the ice above them, showing off the natural curves and ripples in the frozen ceiling of the cave.

There were no words Rachel could think of to express how amazing it was. She could have said beautiful, stunning or awesome, but she needed a word which meant all of those things and even more. It was truly spectacular and totally worth the heart-stopping slip earlier on.

"So, I can tell by the look on your face that you're glad you came now," Jonas said softly.

"And I can see why you never get bored of coming here. It's absolutely magnificent."

Jonas squeezed her hand and then released his grip so that he could begin to explain to the group, accompanied by expansive arm gestures, how the cave was formed.

As Rachel listened to Jonas, she wondered how it would be to hold his hand with no gloves between them. Grabbing her hand at the swimming pool had given her butterflies but not like this. She wanted to feel the strength of his hold against her skin. It had been more than holding hands for her, it had been him protecting her and no-one had ever made her feel that safe before and that made her go weak at the knees.

*

"How was the glacier walking?" asked Gudrun the next day. They had met at the coffee shop to discuss plans for the Design Call.

"It was amazing. I did almost die while I was trying to get up onto the glacier, but apart from that…"

"What? Did you really?"

"Well, it felt like a near-death experience, but I just slipped and Jonas caught me."

"Oh, how romantic! He caught you in his arms."

Considering they barely knew each other, Rachel was amused by how easily they had fallen into a friendship.

"Only because he had to. It wouldn't look good if one of his guests plunged to their death on an excursion."

"True. Lucky he was close enough to catch you in the first place." Gudrun said with wide eyes, trying to elicit more information.

"Yes, it was. Right, where are we going to start with this Design Call then."

There was nothing else to tell. Jonas was a really nice guy and yes, if Rachel was honest, she was attracted to him, but she was struggling with feeling like that. After all, she was with Adam. More than that, she had come away partly to try and reignite the spark between her and Adam. Jonas was so different. Not that she should be comparing them but if she did, all of the things she wished Adam was, Jonas was. How did she even know that? She had only been in the company of Jonas for a total of about six hours. She didn't know anything about him. She had Adam. She didn't *need* to know anything.

That evening, Rachel was on a high. Gudrun had had some great ideas about the Design Call and between them, they had planned a solid programme of work for themselves until the store opened. It was a great feeling to have the first job on the schedule underway and to have an enthusiastic and capable colleague to share the load with.

To reward herself for having such a productive day, Rachel planned to have a relaxing evening at the pool followed by a glass of wine or two in her hotel room. The snow clouds had cleared so Rachel lay in the salt pool gazing at the stars, hoping for a glimpse of the Northern Lights while reminding herself about how unlikely it would be.

When the clouds re-appeared, she decided to get out which meant a few horrible seconds of snow landing on her bare skin as she walked as fast as she could to get back inside. As she almost reached the door to the changing rooms she heard someone shout her name and saw that Jonas was sat in the warm 'socialising' pool. Being so cold that she couldn't bear to stay out in the open even long enough to say hello, she quickly changed direction and ducked into the water next to him, her frozen feet thanking her immediately.

"Hi, Jonas! So, this is a Friday night out for you, is it?" she teased him.

"Well, the start of it. We're going into town afterwards." He gestured to the ledge opposite and one of his friends grinned over at them. "I spotted you in the salt pool but we haven't made it over there yet. I wonder if you'd like to come for a drink with us tonight? We're going to Islenski Barinn, it is very close to your hotel, just off

Laugavegur."

"Oh."

Rachel didn't know what to say. Rather, she knew what she *wanted* to say because she did quite fancy an actual night out with actual people to talk to, especially if those people included Jonas. On the other hand, although she felt like she knew Jonas fairly well now, she felt awkward about going out with a group of his friends too. And yet again, what should have been her overriding reason for saying no, Adam.

"It's just me and these guys." He nodded towards the three men sat opposite. "This is Olafur, who you know from the airport, Siggi and Brun, this is my friend Rachel, she is here from the UK, working for a few weeks."

He made it sound like they'd been friends for ages, which Rachel loved.

"Ah, Rachel who was locked in the shop?" asked Brun.

Rachel blushed and nodded.

They each shook her hand and said it was nice to meet her, and one of them, Siggi, the cheekiest looking of them said, "Come on, Rachel, we can show you the best places to party in town!"

Jonas looked at her apologetically, "Our nights out are not that wild anymore, I'm afraid we are a little old for that now." He grinned at Siggi, who just rolled his eyes. "So, you'll come?"

"Yes, that'd be great. Thank you. I might go back to the hotel to get ready. Could I meet you there later?"

"How about I call to the hotel for you when we are back in town?"

Rachel was so relieved that he had suggested that. She would have dreaded going into the bar by herself. She did it at home all the time, especially if she was meeting Adam because he was invariably late, but for some reason doing it in another country seemed scarier.

"That would be great, thanks. Well, I'll see you later then."

Rachel slid off the bench but kept crouched under the water until she had to stand up to make the cold, mercifully short dash to the changing room.

15

Fortunately, despite her packing issues in London, Rachel had managed to bring something to wear other than practical warm clothes. The choice for her first night out on the town was between her trusty Orla Kiely dress, although she worried it would be too conspicuous with its bright floral print and she certainly didn't want to stand out, or her stretch black brocade dress which was round-necked, sleeveless and had a knee-length full skirt.

As Jonas had said the bar was only across the street and around the corner, Rachel didn't have to worry about what was going to go best with snow boots; she would go all out and wear actual shoes. She decided on the black brocade dress, black opaque tights, her black patent chunky brogues and a mustard-coloured cardigan. She felt like herself again after days of wearing thermals and boots.

Just as she was putting her lipstick on, the receptionist rang the room to say that Jonas was downstairs. Grabbing her coat, phone and purse, she skipped down the stairs and found Jonas waiting beside the fire in the lobby. He looked slightly smarter than she'd seen him look before and when he kissed her on the cheek, he smelled fantastic.

"Wow, you look amazing," he said, instantly making her blush.

"Thanks. Any excuse to put a dress on."

He was alone, his friends having gone ahead to get a table. They walked the short distance to the bar and even though it took less than two minutes, Rachel had to do her coat right up and pull her gloves on because it was so cold.

The bar was fantastic. It was quite dark and was playing good music but not so loudly that you couldn't talk. Jonas's friends had managed to get a big table next to one of the windows which looked out to the street. They already had bottles of beer on the table, including one for Rachel.

"Is this beer okay, Rachel?" asked Olafur. "One of us will drink it if you want something else?"

"No, it's great, thanks. You all speak really good English, which I am very grateful for!" They laughed and all held up their beers to 'cheers' each other. "Skál!"

They were so easy to get along with, so welcoming and friendly. Rachel heard all about how they knew each other, which was a mixture of meeting at primary school and secondary school, all about their jobs, their families, everything. They all lived in or around Reykjavik, Olafur was Gudrun's boyfriend, Brun had a partner, and Siggi was a happy bachelor judging from the flirting that went on with most of the women in the vicinity of the table.

"So, you are Gudrun's Olafur. Is Gudrun coming?" Rachel asked Olafur.

"No, she has gone to see her parents for the weekend. I did not realise you were working with Gudrun. Jonas told me."

"It's a small world, this city," said Rachel, smiling at him.

"Yes, it is. Nothing happens without everyone knowing and everyone knows everyone. That can be good and bad." Olafur gave a wry smile.

Olafur and Jonas talked to Rachel about her work at the shop and they chatted about their business too before Olafur turned to talk to Brun, and Rachel and Jonas were left to talk on their own.

"What are your plans for the weekend?" Jonas asked, taking a sip of his beer as he waited for her to answer.

"Hmm, I don't know. What should I see in town that I haven't already?"

Rachel was about four bottles of beer in and she and Jonas were sat next to each other and had, throughout the evening, gradually moved closer together. Rachel hadn't given it a second thought, she was having a great time. It was so nice to be out, having a drink, she felt like she was on holiday.

"Well, you could go up the Hallgrímskirkja tower? You know, the white church at the top of the street next to Laugavegur? It has a very good view of the city."

"Good idea, I know where that is, it's on the road where the wool shop is," she said, pleased to be able to demonstrate local knowledge.

"The wool shop?" he looked at her, amusement playing in his eyes.

"Yep, I'm knitting a hat. It's a bit like your hat. I saw it and I'm knitting it," she said proudly, hitting the table to emphasise her point.

"I thought that wool was for your mum."

"It was but I needed a hat and… you know," she shrugged.

"So, you like my hat?" he said leaning in towards her, looking right into her eyes, still smiling.

"I do, it is by far the nicest hat I have ever seen and I wanted one the same."

"I would have given you mine if you'd told me that. I've got lots of hats."

The beer and the euphoria of actually being out with people had blinded Rachel to what she would normally, if she was sober, realise was blatant flirting by both of them and even if she'd had the wherewithal to notice, right at this moment she didn't care.

Jonas leaned in and softly kissed her on the lips. It wasn't a lingering kiss but it was nice and if it had lingered she might not have minded. However, it was enough of a kiss to break through the moment and bring her to her senses.

"Sorry Jonas," she said slowly pulling away and shifting herself just a tiny bit further away from him, "I can't." In that instant, she felt quite sad about it.

"No, *I'm* sorry Rachel. I know you've got a boyfriend, I shouldn't have." He rubbed his hand over his chin and sighed.

"It's alright, let's just forget it."

Gently, she leaned into him, giving him a friendly shove.

"That is easier to say than to do."

"Easier said than done."

"Exactly, thank you." He smiled ruefully, without meeting her eye.

Rachel reached up and touched his cheek. "If things were different…"

What else could she say? She was so confused… and so drunk.

Even so, she knew it was not the time. All she could do was leave. She stood up and put her coat on. Jonas stood up too, his hands in his pockets and watched as she zipped her coat and pulled her gloves on.

He leaned in and pecked her on the cheek. "I will walk you back."

"No, it's fine, it's only around the corner. But thank you. And thank you for asking me out tonight I really enjoyed it."

She turned to leave.

"Things could be different."

She didn't turn back, unsure whether Jonas had said that or whether she had muttered it herself.

16

The morning after, Rachel awoke feeling a little bit worse for wear but not as bad as she had feared. She badly needed tea, water and maybe some toast, but she wouldn't be sure about whether she could stomach the toast until she'd had the tea. It was way past breakfast time so she made some tea in her room and dozed in bed, periodically sipping it until she felt reasonably normal.

What had happened last night? The kiss. There was no question that she had done the right thing by putting a stop to it but at the same time, it had seemed like a natural progression of the evening. If she wasn't with Adam, there wouldn't be an issue. But she was with Adam and was not about to cheat on him. The fact that Jonas made her feel things that Adam never had ought to make her question whether she was with the right person, she knew that, however unappealing the prospect was. But that decision had to be separate from Jonas not *because* of Jonas. Didn't it? But the truth was that she was sorry she had stopped the kiss. It felt great to be the centre of someone's attention again. Desired and attractive; it was exciting.

She called Adam. After the beer-skewed thoughts she'd been having about Jonas, she needed to gain some equilibrium back by talking to Adam but it went straight to his voicemail and continued to every other time she tried calling him over the weekend.

*

On Monday morning Rachel rang Jonas's company to organise a trip for the following weekend when Adam was due to visit. She liked Jonas and wanted to give him her business but at the back of her mind, she was worried that it could be awkward if he was running the excursion. Eventually, she had decided that it was unlikely and asking them to confirm who would lead the excursion seemed like overthinking it. This theory was borne out by the fact that the person who she spoke to wasn't Jonas and reassuringly kept repeating phrases like 'One of our guides...' which lessened the odds in her mind. They were going to be picked up at the hotel early on Saturday morning to go on a Golden Circle tour with a meal at a restaurant and then a Northern Lights excursion after that. Perfect.

Gudrun was due to pick her up after breakfast for a trip they were taking to a designer-maker north of Reykjavik who made felted wool homewares. Rachel was excited about it because it was the first Icelandic designer they would meet and she was desperate to build a stunning portfolio of new stockists to wow the London office. She was waiting in the lobby of the hotel, looking out for Gudrun when her phone rang. It was Anna.

"Anna, hi!"

"Hi Rach, how's it going? Been on any more dates with the hunky Icelander?"

Gudrun pulled up and beeped the horn so Rachel hurried out, still on the phone, mouthing hello and sorry to Gudrun as she got into the car.

"It's going great and it wasn't a date."

"I'm just messing. Have you spoken to Adam?"

"No, I've left a couple of messages on his mobile but he was probably working over the weekend. Why do you ask?"

"Oh, no reason. I saw him - not to talk to - on Friday night and I just wondered if he'd said."

"What would he be saying, Anna?" Rachel said, rolling her eyes at Gudrun who was watching the road but smiling as she listened to Rachel's side of the conversation. "Did he see you getting loved up with someone, finally? Oh, is it that bloke from the bar we went to?"

"No, I don't think he saw me."

"Okay, you've lost me. So, what could he have told me then?"

Anna was silent for a second.

"Anna? Are you there?"

"Oh God, Rach. I saw him but I was hoping he might have said something…"

Rachel had never known Anna to be reticent about anything. Normally she was quite the opposite, so something was going on.

"Bloody hell, Anna! Just spit it out. What?"

"I saw him with a woman. I don't know Rach, maybe she was a client and he was just sucking up to her…"

"Were they kissing or something? What do you mean?"

"They were stood together at this cocktail bar…they looked intimate."

"Do you mean they were kissing?" Rachel asked again, feeling slightly sick. Despite Anna planting the seed about it before she left London, Rachel hadn't seriously imagined Adam would do anything like that in a million years. She'd thought she was being paranoid. Some women were constantly looking over their shoulder, jealous of any attention their partner paid to someone else. Rachel wasn't like that but now she wondered if she had just been oblivious. He barely had time for her, let alone anyone else. Unless that was *why* he had no time for her…

"Anna, were they?" Even as she was asking Anna yet again, Rachel had no idea why the idea of him kissing someone else was the thing she needed to get to the bottom of. She knew well enough after Friday night that it could have been a spur of the moment thing that meant nothing. A kiss was not incontrovertible evidence.

"No, they didn't kiss, at least not when I was there but Rach, they looked *together.* The way they were looking at each other and they were touching each other quite… possessively. I just thought he might have mentioned he was going out with a colleague or client or something?"

"He went out with Jim but that was last week. Were they on their own?"

"I think so, I don't know, Rach. I'm sorry. I feel like an idiot for telling you. It's hardly like I caught them snogging or anything…I just thought you would want to know…or that you'd know who it was or something."

When she hung up, Rachel sat in silence for a few minutes. Maybe she was a client. That was the most likely explanation. Or a potential client. Rachel hated to think that Adam would try and win clients by flirting or anything like that but he was very driven.

"Is everything alright?" asked Gudrun.

"Not really, my friend thinks she saw my boyfriend with another woman." Saying it out loud sounded so ridiculous that Rachel started laughing. "Oh my God! He was out with another *woman*!" She pressed the heels of her hands into her eyes and when she took them away, she was crying. "I just can't believe it. It's so unlike him." Wiping her eyes on a tissue she found in her bag, she composed herself. "Sorry, Gudrun. I don't normally cry when I'm at work."

"It's fine, Rachel." Then a few seconds later, "Do you think it is true?"

"I don't know. Until a couple of weeks ago it had never crossed my mind that Adam would ever cheat on me and now I'm unravelling the last two years in my head wondering whether I've been a complete fool."

"You need to talk to him. There could be a very innocent explanation. Were they kissing?"

Rachel wondered if the kissing part was even relevant. Anna had said they looked 'together' – a kiss or not hardly mattered.

"I'm so sorry, it's none of my business," said Gudrun, misreading Rachel's silence as her being offended.

"I've just had minor hysterics in your car and unless I call Anna back and drive her mad when she feels bad enough already, I need someone else to talk to."

"Fantastic. Talk away. Sorry, I don't mean -"

"Gudrun, really if you're happy to hear it, I'm happy to tell you."

Gudrun took her eyes off the road for a second to smile at Rachel. "Always happy."

"You're right, I do need to talk to him but what do I say? Do I sound him out to see if he tells me first, maybe start by saying that Anna saw him and see what he says? Or just say I know he's been seeing someone."

"Hmm, I would probably try to get him to confess rather than accuse him because then he will be defensive. If you want to stay with him you need to know he is telling you the truth, not keeping secrets. And if he is seeing someone else you probably need to know how long it's been going on or whether he's seen other people before."

"If I want to stay with him," said Rachel quietly. "Before I came here, I felt like things weren't right between us. I don't know whether it was to do with this woman, maybe that was why things hadn't been so good but I thought we needed a break from each other and a chance to miss each other and I really hoped that would make a difference. Now I know that he hasn't been missing me or he was and has filled the void with someone else."

"What were you going to do if nothing changed when you got back?"

"I hadn't thought that far ahead. I suppose I thought it would work and we'd just carry on. But being here has given me space to think and I have been feeling differently and thinking about our relationship and whether he's actually The One."

"You must have thought he was The One in the beginning?"

"I did to start with." Not an emphatic, 'yes'. "There weren't sparks or anything like that. I mean, obviously, I fancied him and I do love him. Is Olafaur The One?"

"Definitely. As soon as I met him I knew. And the first time we touched, it was like electricity."

Gudrun's eyes were sparkling and Rachel could see how much she loved Olafur as she spoke about him. And she knew exactly what Gudrun was talking about because she had felt that spark with Jonas.

"The thing is, it's not as if I haven't been tempted but I just wouldn't do anything like that while I'm with Adam."

Rachel blushed as she thought of the times she'd let her mind wander with thoughts of being with Jonas. But the kiss on Friday night was all him. She had nothing to feel bad about. But if one of Adam's friends had seen her in the bar on Friday night with Jonas and his friends, they might have jumped to a similar conclusion to Anna.

"Adam deserves the benefit of the doubt," she said decisively.

The visit to the designer was a huge success with Rachel and Gudrun placing a big order that would be ready in time for the opening of the shop. It was really important to them both to have some Icelandic stock for the launch and they had also discussed with the designer the possibility of exporting to the Snug shops in the UK.

After all the emotional upheaval of the morning, Rachel was

exhausted and declined Gudrun's offer of a quick dinner when they got back to Reykjavik in favour of room service and an early night. Yet another day had gone by without Adam returning her calls from the weekend. The calls she'd made before Anna's revelation and which now made her feel like an idiot because maybe that was *why* he'd missed them. Despite being desperate to speak to him she really didn't know what to say and hoped that sleeping on it would help. Perhaps he would ring tomorrow and tell her that he'd just secured a new client. Would it be okay then if that's what it was? Was the next phone call between them going to be the end? Once her mind had stopped whirring with possibilities, Rachel fell into a deep sleep.

*

The work at the shop was in full swing now. Rachel and Gudrun spent the next morning taping sheets of protective covering over the beautifully finished floor ready for the onslaught of heating and fire alarm installers.

They'd had some postcards printed with information about the Design Call and once they'd finished at the shop, they strolled around town leaving them in what they hoped were strategic places.

"Have you spoken to Adam?" asked Gudrun as they headed towards the Harpa.

"No, not yet. He's supposed to be coming to visit this weekend so I had wondered whether to leave it until he's here. Perhaps it's better to talk face-to-face."

"True, that probably is better."

"The only thing is, whether he will actually come."

"Why would he not come? He doesn't know that anything is wrong."

"No, not because of that. He's not very good at putting things like that first. If anything came up at work he wouldn't think twice about cancelling."

"But if it's a long-standing arrangement and a holiday, surely not?"

Gudrun looked surprised and for a minute Rachel saw it through Gudrun's eyes and wondered if she was wrong to doubt him. But *any* arrangement she had with Adam couldn't be relied on. That fact was sad but true. And of course, it was natural for Gudrun to be surprised to think that her boyfriend might just not turn up. If Rachel was watching it happen to someone else, she'd think the guy was being a dick for even thinking of not coming on a trip like this when he said he was going to and arrangements had been made. She was too accepting of Adam's behaviour and being distanced from it made that clear to her.

The lack of contact from him, even before Anna's phone call had made Rachel begin to think that he must be snowed under at work. He would work crazy hours and be so distracted that he wouldn't think of sending a text or a quick email to touch base. The fact that she was away, gave him free rein to be even more like that with no-one there to have any expectations of him.

On Wednesday morning Rachel finally had an email from him. It wasn't a phone call but it was something.

Hi Rach, I hope everything is going well over there. Sorry I haven't called in a few days. I had to work all weekend and have been in too late every night to ring you but I'm surprised you haven't called me. Have you been snowed under?! Things here are not great, the Scramble deal has hit a real wall with the contract negotiations. I hope you have good Wi-Fi as I will need to check my emails while I'm there. Can't wait to see you. A x

She typed out a brief reply.

Hi Adam, yes, I've been really busy too. It is going well though, thanks. Hope work calms down enough so you can enjoy the weekend, I'm looking forward to seeing you too. Love you xx

Thank goodness she had no time to dwell on Adam's email. Now that the floor was finished, her mind was buzzing with the schedule, things she needed to add to her to-do list, and things to remember to flag up with Nick or the office. There were just three weeks left before opening now.

There were two guys, John and Rob, plus Nick in the build team. They had started by ripping out anything internally that wasn't staying, things like old pipe coverings, odd bits of fixings in the wall and some wall cladding which harked back to at least the 1970s. It was always a dicey moment; assessing how much work was needed to make the walls good.

The first container from the UK had arrived in Iceland and would be brought to the shop for unloading at 8 am. Because the store was in the heart of the city, container lorries couldn't drive through in the middle of the day. It was full of the fixtures and fittings and all the other fit-out stuff so Nick, John and Rob were going to unload it, then their first job once the heating engineers had finished would be to fit the suspended ceiling which would hide all the service pipes and wires and would give Rachel and Gudrun lots of fixing points for their displays.

It was always a milestone moment when the shop could start being put together again so Rachel had sent some photos to Luisa in London to show her the blank canvas. She was keeping a close eye on how things were progressing, knowing that it was Rachel's first time in sole charge of a project, albeit with plenty of support, and she was pleased with how everything was shaping up.

Despite the change in pace with work, Rachel had made time every evening to relax in her room with her knitting and had actually almost finished her hat. She was secretly thrilled that it would be ready to wear on her excursion with Adam at the weekend. She thought she had done a pretty good job and in a throwback to her childhood, had used bits of all the wool she had left to make a colourful oversized pom-pom for the top. Ta-dah! She took a selfie of herself wearing it and emailed it to her mum and dad.

17

From the minute she woke up on Friday, Rachel had butterflies in her stomach in anticipation of Adam's arrival. They had never been apart for so long and despite her worries about addressing whatever it was Anna had seen, she was looking forward to seeing him, being close to him and, hopefully, enjoying a romantic couple of days. She had checked the weather forecast to make sure there wasn't going to be a snowstorm or anything that would stop flights and it all looked good.

She kept busy all day to try and stop herself from constantly checking the time. Adam's flight was at 6 pm from London City airport so he should make it to the hotel by 10.30 pm at the latest. It seemed like such a long time to have to wait and she wished she had insisted on picking him up just to give her something to do.

At 4 pm she had an email, from Adam's work email address, which made her heart sink.

Rach, so sorry but I'm not going to make my flight. Megan has looked into changing and I can get a flight out later tonight at 10 otherwise in the morning at 8. Will do my best to make the first and will text you later. A x

It was just what she had feared and what she had forced herself not to expect. She felt sick with disappointment and so angry with Adam and with herself because she'd seen it coming but had carried on hoping for the best. He probably still really thought he'd get one of those other flights whereas Rachel knew that if it had come to this already, he wasn't coming.

The thought of spending the weekend alone just made her feel worse. Aside from anything else, she felt robbed of the opportunity to find out from him, face-to-face, what had been going on in London while she'd been away.

After she left the shop, she sat in bed with a glass of wine, angry, silent tears coursing down her face while she went over and over all the times this type of thing had happened before. It had never mattered as much as this before. He had let her down and she had expected it. Why was she still waiting for him to be the kind of man that she wanted him to be when he had shown her so many times that he wasn't? Was she just going to carry on hoping forever? How many times had he surprised her by coming through for her? Apart from the Icebar, which had been exceptional, she couldn't think of a single example. The Icebar. It had been a night of extraordinary behaviour from Adam. A grand gesture before she left or, she wondered now, the result of a guilty conscience.

Throughout the evening, he texted with more apologies and the news that surprise, surprise he wasn't going to fly out that night and probably not in the morning either. Well, if he wasn't coming tonight, she didn't want him to come. If he manned up enough to ring her, she didn't want to speak to him anyway so she switched her phone off.

*

When her alarm woke her at 6 am, she was emotionally drained but with a determination not to let what had happened ruin her weekend. She was still going to go on the excursion. It would take her mind off things and besides, she had been dying to see more of the country and it could be her only opportunity now that things were getting busier at the shop.

She waited in the foyer of the hotel, layered to the max in thermals, waterproof trousers, snow boots, her down jacket, souvenir gloves and best of all, her new hat. Despite having been hoping that Jonas wouldn't be running the excursion, now that Adam wasn't going Rachel couldn't help hoping that it would be him.

The minibus pulled up and the driver hopped out to greet her and open the door to the back of the bus. He explained that they had one more pick up to make and then they'd be on their way. It wasn't Jonas but Rachel reasoned that in the circumstances perhaps she was better off with her own company.

As the bus made its way through the narrow streets of the town centre in the dark of the morning, a worry began to niggle at her. Her phone was still off, although she had brought it with her in the breast pocket of her coat purely for taking photos. Despite being determined not to care anymore about whether Adam was going to turn up or not, she couldn't help but worry that maybe he had decided to get the morning flight. He'd arrive and she wouldn't be there. He knew she had planned the excursion today, she had emailed him the details, but she was sure he wouldn't expect that she had decided to go alone. But then why did it matter? The fact was, she had no idea either way and that was down to him. He could sort himself out.

The bus stopped at a hotel on the outskirts of town to pick up two more people, a couple clearly in the throes of a romantic weekend themselves, which only made Rachel feel angry with Adam again, so she left her phone where it was and soon forgot to worry about what Adam was doing when the driver and tour guide, Einar, introduced himself over the minibus tannoy and began to tell them a potted history of Iceland as they made their way to the first stop of the day, Thingvellir National Park.

Einar turned off the main road and followed a narrow track to a car park which had a couple of low wooden buildings to the left. He informed them that they were the information centre and the toilets. Everyone piled out of the minibus and wandered over to look at the information boards on the other side of the car park.

Rachel was standing at what felt like the top of a cliff, looking out over a snow-covered plateau where there was a small cluster of white clapboard buildings. Looking to the left, according to the information board, what Rachel was looking at was the bottom of the rift between the tectonic plates of America and Europe. It was very easy to make out and completely amazing to see. She carried on along the path and downwards, between the rift, just fascinated to think that she was walking along the gap between two continents.

She had to succumb and turn her phone on so that she could use the camera to capture the spectacular scenery. Unsurprisingly, there was no mobile signal in the middle of nowhere which was an immense relief as she still wasn't sure what she was going to say to Adam and if there had been a text from him, she'd have felt compelled to reply. As it was, she enjoyed taking endless pictures of the dramatic scenery, able to keep ignoring what she knew she was going to have to face sooner or later. Later was better.

The rest of the day was one endless photo opportunity, visiting one spectacular natural phenomenon after another. The highlight for Rachel was visiting the Great Geysir although it didn't erupt regularly anymore, it was a smaller geyser, Strokkur, which erupted every twenty minutes or so and was the main attraction these days. It was mesmerising to watch and after a couple of eruptions, you knew to look for the way the water swelled which signalled an eruption so Rachel managed to get a decent photo of it in action.

It was so much colder out in the countryside than it was in Reykjavik that Rachel was glad of her new hat to keep her toasty even if it did make her forehead itch like mad. The snow was deeper too and she would not have wanted to be Einar, driving on barely visible roads, the edges marked by yellow sticks because you couldn't tell where they were otherwise. Scary. She tried not to look out at the road ahead while they were driving along because it gave her the heebie-jeebies.

At the last stop, an amazing waterfall called Gullfoss, Einar took her aside to let her know the arrangements for the rest of the day. Rachel was the only person booked for the dinner and Northern Lights excursion so the minibus would drop her off at the restaurant and then the Northern Lights tour would pick her up later on. She was in half a mind to say forget it because she didn't want to eat dinner alone, but Einar said that there was a very good chance that the aurora would show that evening and that was the deciding factor for her.

On the way to the restaurant, the dusk and the hum of the engine lulled Rachel to sleep and only the minibus door sliding open when they arrived woke her.

From the outside, the restaurant reminded her of a lake-side house or ski-lodge. It was built like a log cabin with a wrap-around veranda which was strung with fairy lights and there were floor-to-ceiling glass windows which showed the inviting looking interior. It may have been near a lake but in the dark, it was impossible to tell and it appeared that yet again, Rachel was in the middle of nowhere with nothing else to be seen apart from a coach in the car park.

If Adam had been with her and they had been expecting a romantic dinner for two at this restaurant they would have been disappointed, but for Rachel, it was completely perfect. In the centre of the room was a huge circular fire pit, built upon a stone surround underneath an enormous canopied chimney flue. It was surrounded by two circles of tables and benches and there were small wooden stools placed closer to the fire where it appeared that people were barbecuing meat on sticks.

Rachel was shown to a table on the circle closest to the fire which already had another six people sat there. They were very welcoming and were in high spirits as most people seemed to be. The atmosphere was fabulous, anything but romantic, but perfect for that particular evening.

The menu was a list of various platters of meat and you could choose what kinds of meat you wanted to try. They came with side orders if you wanted; various potato dishes, salads or breads.

The protocol seemed to be that you skewered your meat or whatever you had chosen, barbecued it yourself and then ate it back at your table. Oh my God, Adam would have loved it, thought Rachel, her heart softening a tiny bit as she thought of him.

Having ordered a large glass of red wine and a platter of meat which included lamb, beef and smoked puffin which Rachel felt a little reluctant about trying, although most of the platters had something on them that she wouldn't normally eat (whale was definitely off her list of things to try) it felt like part of the point of being there.

When her food arrived, she skewered up her first batch and found a stool to sit on around the fire. There were some huge logs in the centre which were burning well and every so often a guy with a long rake would bring some of the hottest embers to the edges of the fire to keep the barbecue going. Having no idea what she was doing or how long the meat would take to cook, she just copied what other people were doing, assuming that they probably knew. There was a sense of camaraderie around the fire, everyone was chatting, comparing meats, speculating on the best way to eat them, rare or well-done; Rachel thoroughly enjoyed herself.

The meat was absolutely delicious, so tender and full of flavour. She ate it straight from the skewer interspersing it with bites of salad and beautiful bread. What a fantastic meal, easily the best she'd had for a long time anywhere, let alone in Iceland.

With another half an hour to go before she was being picked up she ordered another glass of wine because as content as she was to sit and watch everyone else cooking their meat, it was nice to have something to sip on.

There was a tap on her shoulder and she turned to see Jonas standing behind her, togged up to the eyes in a bigger coat than normal and holding his hat in his hands.

"Jonas, what are you doing here?" she said in surprise.

"I've come to meet you for the Northern Lights excursion." He smiled and any awkwardness she might have felt with it being the first time they had seen each other since the kiss, disappeared.

"Well, it's probably just as well that Adam didn't make his flight after all. It's just me."

"Einar told me. He rang to check the aurora forecast and said that it was just one person for the tour instead of two." His smile faded into a look of concern. "He missed his flight? Are you okay?"

"Yes, I'm fine. He had to work."

She wasn't about to start criticising Adam to Jonas, although it would have been easy to. She was desperate to talk to someone about it, Anna or Gudrun, but it would be disloyal to talk to Jonas and however angry Rachel was with Adam, she hadn't lost all sense of reason.

"There's plenty of time, so finish your drink and I'll be waiting outside when you're ready."

She saw him stop to talk to the manager on his way out. They were clearly friends. Rachel wondered whether Jonas knew almost everyone; maybe that's what happened in a small place like this. She liked the thought of him having a huge circle of friends and acquaintances; it matched her impression of him being a friendly, warm and easy-going person.

She didn't rush to finish her wine, partly because she didn't want the amazing experience in the restaurant to be over and partly because she was inexplicably nervous about being alone with Jonas. Good grief.

She was immensely relieved that Adam wasn't here now but maybe if he had been, Jonas wouldn't have chosen to be their tour guide. Would she have managed to act normally around Jonas with

Adam there and would Adam have thought it was weird that she was friends with him? Moot points, Rachel told herself sternly as she finished her wine and went outside to find Jonas.

Jonas jumped out of the jeep as he saw her leave the restaurant and held the door open for her.

"I love your hat," he said. "It is just like mine. I'm missing this bit though." He reached up and flicked the pom-pom.

"Thanks, not quite to the same standard as yours." Despite her modesty, she was thrilled that he'd noticed.

"I would not know the difference." His eyes were shining as he closed the door after her.

Rachel's eyes were already glued to the skies – there didn't seem to be many stars which surprised her as she had been expecting a clear sky.

As if reading her mind, Jonas said, "We will drive towards Reykjavik and we should find clearer skies on the way but it is cloudier than we expected." He was looking up at the sky himself, his brow furrowed.

They set off, sitting in silence with Rachel still staring in hopeful wonder at the sky looking for any glimpse of the Northern Lights while at the same time not sure what she was looking for unless it was a spectacular display like you saw in travel magazines.

It started to snow very lightly. She looked over at Jonas who was still frowning as he focused on the road ahead. It was not the kind of place Rachel would want to drive in at night, or in the day come to that, so she wasn't surprised at how hard he was concentrating. The lying snow made everything brighter but when she wasn't looking at the sky she was watching the poles that marked the edge of the road as if her life depended on it.

"Is everything alright, Jonas?" she asked, slightly anxiously, mainly because he was looking concerned and she had never seen him anything but relaxed and happy.

"Well, the forecast was not for snow, so it is a surprise." He pulled over to the side of the road and leaned across her to retrieve a large phone from the glove compartment. "There's no signal here," he said gesturing the windscreen, "so we always carry satellite phones in case of an emergency."

"Is this an emergency?" she said, alarmed.

"I'm going to call to find out the latest weather forecast. Don't worry."

Keen as she was to know what was going on, Jonas's side of the conversation was no use to her at all as it was in Icelandic, but she could tell from his face that the weather forecast was not what he wanted to hear.

He finished the call, laid the phone on his lap and then pulled back onto the road. Rachel was looking at him, waiting for him to tell her what was going on but he kept looking forward, fixed on the road ahead.

"So, is the Northern Lights trip off then?" she asked when it was clear that he wasn't going to explain the phone call.

"Yes, the forecast is not good, there is a snowstorm passing over so we won't be able to get back to Reykjavik tonight."

18

"What do you mean? We're in the middle of nowhere, how did you not know about a massive snowstorm?"

Rachel couldn't believe that they were going to be stranded in the *actual* middle of *actually* nowhere. In the freezing cold.

"Rachel, the weather is very changeable in Iceland. At this time of year, it can be unpredictable. It isn't dangerous, it's just that we can't use the mountain road until the storm passes and there is no other way back but I have arranged the use of a cabin for the night. I have asked for a message to be left at your hotel as well, just in case."

He sounded so calm and hadn't looked over at her at all, he just scrutinised the road ahead as the snow became heavier.

"I haven't got anything with me and we're in the middle of nowhere!"

"Look," he said firmly, "there is no need to panic. Olafur's on the other end of the emergency satellite phone and his cousin has a summer cabin near here. I have directions and we can use it for the night. We will be safe." He took his hand off the steering wheel, found her hand and squeezed it. "Please, don't worry," he glanced briefly at her, his eyes imploring her to trust him, "I'll look after you."

Jonas turned off the road onto a smaller track. There were no signposts but it was the first turning they had seen for miles so maybe it was the right way. As they drove further along, the shapes of buildings, all in darkness, loomed out of the thickening snowfall.

On this less travelled road, the jeep was starting to struggle, the wheels were spinning and all they could see in the headlights was horizontal snow, so Jonas suggested that as they were so close, they should walk the last part.

They did their coats up, pulled on their hats and gloves and prepared to enter the blizzard. Rachel jumped down into the snow which was easily a foot deep already. Jonas came round to her, took her hand and led the way, battling into the wind, barely able to see where they were heading, towards the cluster of cabins. He made her wait while he checked each in turn until he found the one that belonged to Olafur's family, then he waved her over, "Rachel, it's here!"

By the time Rachel had got inside and taken her boots off, Jonas was already busy lighting the wood-burning stove. It was freezing but it was more than preferable to being outside in the wind and snow. The cabin was quite bijou with a comfortable looking sofa covered with throws and cushions which faced the fire. To the right, separated from the lounge by a breakfast bar was a tiny kitchen right next to French windows where the snow accumulation was deep against the glass.

Jonas soon had the fire roaring using logs from a pile which was artfully stacked at the side of the fireplace. The only other light came from a few candles that he'd lit on the breakfast bar. It was very atmospheric, and although it was a bit frightening to be stranded like this, Rachel couldn't help thinking that it was just another authentic taste of Iceland that she was getting to experience and now that they were safe and almost warm, she was feeling pretty relaxed about the whole thing.

She curled up in the corner of the sofa with a throw over her watching the fire blaze. Jonas had found a kettle and was boiling it up on the stove. He sat down in the opposite corner of the sofa and tucked his legs underneath him, watching the fire as well.

"Are you warm enough?"

"Yes, it's really cosy. It's a lovely cabin." She was nervous. It was undeniably romantic in this cabin, she still had a fair amount of red wine in her system and looking at Jonas in the candlelight, having heroically and calmly saved them from the storm, she had reason to be nervous.

"I think it might be best if we both sleep in here on the sofa bed to keep warm, the bedroom will be freezing. I'll find some more blankets and pillows in a minute."

Rachel didn't say anything, surmising that it was probably the most sensible thing to do given that she definitely didn't want to move away from the fire and she couldn't expect Jonas to either. Besides, as it was far too cold to think about undressing, they'd have their clothes on, so what was the harm.

Jonas got up and took the kettle into the kitchen with him, returning a minute later with steaming mugs of something similar to Horlicks. He put some more logs on the fire and they sat in comfortable silence again for a few minutes on the sofa, sipping their drinks and staring into the fire.

"Has this ever happened to you before?" she asked.

"Once, about six years ago. It was on the way back from a day excursion to a glacier, the one we went to actually. I was leading a group of eight and the weather turned before we could get to the main road. Because we were in a minibus it was worse to drive even with snow tyres so I knew I wouldn't get very far. We were lucky; there was a decent hostel in a town nearby and we just about made it there."

The firelight flickered on his face as he spoke.

"What would have happened if we didn't have this cabin tonight?"

"I would have driven back to the restaurant. I expect the coach party are still there, they wouldn't have set out in this blizzard. It could have been a good night." He turned to her and smiled.

"It was an amazing place. I've never been anywhere like it before. I'm sorry not to have seen the Northern Lights tonight but the restaurant and all the other things I've done today have been brilliant."

"I'm glad you had a good day. You've seen a bit of the real Iceland tonight though. Not many tourists get that chance."

"The other day felt like the real Iceland too when I nearly fell off that glacier. Hopefully, not many tourists get that bit either."

"No, you are right," Jonas grinned, "you seem to be having quite a unique experience."

"Well, I love it. And I'd never have come here if it wasn't for work, it just wouldn't have occurred to me. Most people I know head to Greece and Spain on holiday and that seems so boring in comparison."

"It certainly isn't boring, there are interesting things to see in those countries too, it's just that most people head to the coasts. There are always interesting things, Rachel, you just have to take the time to find them."

The fire was roaring now and the warmth from it was spreading slowly around the room.

"But you see things differently and I love that. You take time to notice and I've only just begun to try but it gives me an enormous sense of everything being right with the world and makes me feel uplifted at the same time. I mean, today could have been rubbish." Jonas raised his eyebrows and she quickly added, "From a personal point of view, obviously not the excursion. But it was a strangely perfect day in the end."

"Strangely perfect," Jonas murmured.

Having finished their drinks, Rachel rinsed the mugs while Jonas fought the sofa bed into submission and found some sheets and pillows from the bedroom. He put some more logs on the fire while she stood watching the snow fall deeper and deeper against the window.

"Do you think we'll be able to leave tomorrow?"

"We'll have to wait and see. There wasn't a big snowfall forecast, I think it will stop soon and as long as we can get back to the main road we should be able to get over the mountain road by midday. I will phone the office in the morning to see what the situation is. Don't worry, Rachel. We'll get back sometime tomorrow, I'm sure."

Jonas had started removing layers of clothes while he was talking until he was down to a long-sleeved top and leggings, presumably his thermals.

"No, I'm not worried, it's fine."

If they were snowed in she wouldn't be sorry, she thought, as she began removing some of her layers. There were far worse situations to be in.

They both got into bed. Jonas had put a separate set of blankets for each of them which seemed to be an Icelandic thing to do. The double bed in the hotel had two single duvets on it, so she knew he wasn't just being careful to keep them apart.

They lay in the darkness which was punctuated only by the

flicker of the fire. Rachel pondered on how odd it was to be sharing a bed with someone she didn't know all that well and she felt funny about being asleep in front of him for some reason. Maybe he would fall asleep first.

"Are you okay?" His voice came softly out of the dark.

"Yes. Are you?"

"Yes. Are you warm enough?"

Rachel snuggled under the blankets a bit more. "Yes, thanks."

"Good, I will try and keep the fire going. Night Rachel."

"Night, Jonas. Thank you for everything."

"You are welcome."

Rachel's eyes closed and she began to think back over the day. She'd enjoyed it so much and it was the perfect end. Well, perhaps not perfect. Seeing the Northern Lights would have been perfect but being here with Jonas, cosy in a snowstorm was a close second.

She wondered what the day would have been like if Adam had come. She probably wouldn't be here now, that was for sure. Would they have had a great time? Would it have been as much fun given what Anna had told her? Was that the real reason he didn't come? He had let her down before because of work but this felt like another level, more than just a broken promise or missed flight. It was more like a rejection this time and she'd never felt rejected by him before. Yes, she'd been shuffled down his priority list on more than one occasion, but never rejected.

Being apart wasn't making things better between them. It hadn't made Adam miss her because if he did he would have come.

Rachel let out a sigh and then felt Jonas's hand reach for hers between the covers. He squeezed her hand in his and then didn't let go. Neither of them spoke but when Rachel went to move position he pulled her to him and hugged her to his chest.

She could feel his heart beating against her cheek as he cradled her head to him. He gently stroked a finger across her forehead as if there were a stray hair he was brushing aside. All she could hear was his heart and the fire crackling periodically. She could feel his breath rising under her and then warm against the top of her head as he breathed out.

They lay still, in silence, Jonas not releasing his hold. Rachel felt safer, warmer and more comforted than she could ever remember. She tilted her head to look at him, seeing from the light of the fire that he had his eyes shut but feeling her move, he briefly opened them, met her gaze, smiled sleepily then closed them again, pulling her even closer. She shifted slightly so that her face was next to his and gently kissed his lips. It took him a second to respond but he softly kissed her back, hooking his fingers behind her neck and stroking her cheek with his thumb.

In that moment, Rachel didn't care about Adam, she wasn't even thinking about him anymore, she just cared about this. This stolen, unexpected night in the wilderness of this beautiful country. Just her, Jonas and the warmth of the fire.

19

The following day Rachel woke to an empty bed. The fire was still roaring and she could see that Jonas's boots and clothes were missing so she guessed he must have gone out to check on the jeep and have a look at the road. The snow had stopped, giving way to a glorious winter day of blue skies and sunshine.

Jonas came back in as she was getting dressed, stamping his feet and rubbing his hands together.

"I'm guessing it's cold out there?" Rachel pulled her sweater over her head and then combed her hair through with her fingers in the hope of making it look reasonable.

"Yes, very cold, but it is a beautiful day. Shall I make some breakfast?"

He began rummaging through the cupboards, managing to find long-life milk, instant coffee and some porridge oats.

"I spoke to the office and the mountain road should be open from midday. This road is bad though so I will have to dig around the jeep so we can turn it around and then we'll take it steadily back to the main road."

He passed Rachel a milky coffee and stirred the porridge on the stove.

"I can help you dig. I've never seen snow this deep before."

"This is not deep. If it was deep, we wouldn't be digging around the jeep, we'd be digging to try and find it." He flashed her a smile before he went back to dishing up the porridge.

Rachel loved how easy it was to be with him. Yet again, she

found herself inadvertently comparing him to Adam, thinking that she couldn't imagine Jonas ever sulking and shutting her out. Then she reminded herself that she really didn't know him that well, although she already felt as if he was an old friend.

"Thank you, that would be great. It'll take us a while."

The coffee was lovely and although Rachel wasn't a fan of porridge, she thought it would be wise to equip herself with a 'Ready Brek' glow before she braved the cold.

They left the cabin just as they'd found it, minus a little bit of food, drink and some logs. Jonas left a thank-you note and a few thousand Krona to pay for the food and wood then they got their boots on and locked the door behind them.

The jeep wasn't far along the road; it had felt further when they were battling through the blizzard in the darkness. The side road they were on was quite narrow, you could see the slight dips in the snow where the ditch was at either side of the road and there was a good forty to fifty centimetres of snow, more in places where it had drifted.

They shovelled the jeep's wheels free of snow and then worked to make a space around it so they could turn. Even with snow tyres, Jonas reckoned the snow was too deep for them to grip effectively.

"Rachel, are you digging?" Jonas called from the other side of the jeep.

"Yes, why?"

"I think you need a break!" he said, just as a snowball hit her on the back.

"Aagghhh! You cheeky sod!"

She had already cast the shovel aside and was busy making a snowball to retaliate with when another one hit her, again on the back. She stood up and couldn't see Jonas but she could hear him laughing.

"I'll get you!" she shouted, taking the opportunity to make a couple of extra snowballs before the next onslaught.

Positioning herself strategically, she lobbed one over the roof of the jeep and knew she had missed Jonas when she heard him laughing all the more loudly. The next one was more successful and she heard him shriek.

"Okay! You got me!"

"Was it you? Because it sounded like a little girl shrieking!"

"Very funny!"

Rachel lobbed another one.

"*Vopnahlé*! I give up!" called Jonas.

"Already? You must have had more snowball fights than me, which gives you a major advantage and you want to give up?"

As she stooped to make another snowball, Jonas came around the jeep and stood in front of her, snow on his hat – evidence of a direct hit. He held out his hand which she took. He pulled her towards him as if he was going to kiss her. She felt his hands on her upper arms, his hold taking her breath away. Then he swiped her feet from under her and half pushed, half lowered her into a huge snowdrift.

"Jonas!" shrieked Rachel. "Oh, my God, that's not a truce!"

"*You* didn't say truce," he said, proceeding to fall backwards so that he was lying next to her. His eyes were twinkling and she was sure hers looked just the same. "I think this has been the best excursion I've ever been on."

His voice was soft and Rachel just wanted this moment to be perfect. She wanted to be able to lose herself in the feelings which were suddenly overwhelming her, but she knew she had to settle things one way or the other with Adam and despite being desperate to do the right thing by sorting things out with him independently of any other feelings she may have, that was proving to be more challenging with every minute she spent with Jonas. But she owed it to Adam and their relationship to hear his side of whatever story there was.

"Me too," she said brightly, attempting to get to her feet. She looked at Jonas, hoping to convey all these things she was thinking without having to say anything. He looked resigned and smiled ruefully.

"This jeep won't dig itself out, we'd better get on," he said, hauling himself to his feet and pulling Rachel up beside him.

"Thank you," she said softly, squeezing his hand. She knew he understood.

Finally, they got into the jeep, Jonas expertly manoeuvred it around and they crept slowly along the road. Once they reached the main road the snow was quite compacted from other vehicles so it was relatively easy to drive on. As they approached the city, the road rose over the mountains. Despite the calm, winter wonderland lower down, at the top of the mountain the wind was blowing the lying snow in great sheets of powder across the road reducing the visibility dramatically. It was frightening. The jeep was being buffeted by the strong wind and Jonas was struggling to keep the windscreen clear and to keep on the right side of the road. It was an immense relief when they started descending again, out of the wind and away from the treacherous drops on either side of the road.

Jonas stopped right outside Rachel's hotel and she gave him a quick kiss on the cheek before she said goodbye and jumped out.

"Hey Rachel," called Jonas after her. "Maybe we could do that again sometime?"

"Maybe."

Maybe they could.

The receptionist greeted her and said that there was a message for her to call Adam. She went up to the room and turned her phone back on. There were a few missed calls and two voicemails from Adam, one of which was an apology for not coming and another where he sounded quite worried, saying that he knew about the storm and that she should ring him when she got back.

Although she was still cross with him, she didn't want him worrying about her so she took a deep breath and called him, having no idea what she was going to say.

He picked up really quickly. "Rachel, hi, are you alright?"

He sounded concerned and from his voice, she could picture him frowning as he spoke.

"I'm fine. I just got back."

"The tour company said you got caught in a snowstorm. What happened?"

"It was very heavy snow so we couldn't make it back from the excursion. We stayed in someone's cabin. It was fine."

She couldn't help but be brief, annoyed that he hadn't started off by explaining why he didn't come. Or by apologising.

"How many of you were there?"

"Just two of us."

"Just you and the guide?"

"Well, there would have been three of us but someone didn't turn up."

He was silent for a second and a pang of guilt hit her. It was a bit below the belt but nevertheless, true.

"Okay. Point taken." He paused before he said, "You don't know how sorry I am that I didn't make it this weekend, especially now."

Rachel deliberately didn't fill the silence, forcing him to continue.

"I would have lost my job, Rach. A year of working on the Scramble deal all came to a head this weekend. It wasn't supposed to be this weekend, it should have been finished already, but there was nothing I could do." Another pause. "Could I come out this weekend instead? My ticket -"

"No. I'll be working every weekend now. It was the only chance."

She wasn't prepared to give herself a week of emotional stress about whether he would or wouldn't turn up. Yes, it would be better to see him, to talk things through and goodness knows, this phone call wasn't the right time to do that, but it was too much. It was better to just concentrate on work now. She *needed* to concentrate on work.

"Rach, I need you to know how sorry I am. If there had been any way around it, I would have been there."

He was starting to sound desperate now. Rachel pictured him running his hand through his hair in frustration. She was glad. This sorry was no different to any other sorry she'd had from him before. Work was his excuse this time as it had been every time.

"Look, Adam. I know you think it was unavoidable, but for me, it's another let-down on a long list of let-downs and because of work again. But it's worse this time because I'm here. It's so hard to do this over the phone."

"I know you're angry with me, you have every right to be but I will make it up to you when you get back, I promise. Please believe me, I know how much I've let you down and hurt you," he said gently.

If it was just that he hadn't come, Rachel would have forgiven him, she would have fallen for his charm but the words didn't touch her this time. This time, they sounded hollow because all she could picture was him with the other woman.

"Look, I know we need to talk but I can't do it now." Suddenly overwhelmed with tiredness she said, "I'm too tired to think. I'll ring you tomorrow night." Trying not to cry because it would make everything worse, she simply said, "Bye."

"I love you, Rach."

She ended the call without saying anything else.

Then the tears did come. Great big sobs, partly because she was tired but mostly because she was feeling emotionally drained after the phone call with Adam and with managing the conflicting feelings she had for Adam and Jonas.

Her phone pinged a few minutes later, it was a text from Gudrun.

Heard about your night in the snowstorm! Shall we meet for coffee in the morning? 10 am Te & Kaffi? G x

Perfect. Rachel xx

20

By the next morning Rachel was resolute. She'd had a good cry and mulled everything over for what seemed like the entire night so although she felt exhausted, at the same time she was feeling refreshed and purposeful. She had been distracted by Adam and Jonas and the excitement of being in Iceland but she was here to work and to do the best job she could of launching her first-ever Snug store, and that was what she was going to do.

She found Gudrun sitting at the table in the back corner of Te & Kaffi. After ordering a latte and a chocolate croissant, she sat down opposite Gudrun, who looked more animated and enthusiastic than normal.

"So, tell me what happened in the snowstorm."

"Well, the forecast hadn't said it was going to snow and…"

"No! Not that part, I know all that, Olafur told me. I want to know what happened in the cabin."

Now Rachel knew why Gudrun looked so perky. She was practically out of her chair in her impatience to know the details.

"Oh, God. Look, nothing happened. Well, not nothing but not *that*."

Gudrun's face told Rachel that wasn't going to be an acceptable explanation.

"Okay. I'm going to tell you because, to be honest, I don't know what to do and I need to get it off my chest but then, that's it. We are working our arses off. Deal?"

"Yes!" Then feigning innocence, "I am just trying to help you,

Rachel. I think if you can talk to me, you will be clearer about your feelings?"

"Maybe. So, Jonas and I ended up in the cabin. And because it was cold, we slept in the same bed but with separate covers. And we snuggled. He's the perfect gentleman."

"He *is* perfect. Completely perfect for you."

"No, I mean he is absolutely the loveliest man, but I have Adam."

"Who has been cheating on you."

"We don't know that yet," said Rachel reasonably.

"So, you haven't spoken to him?" asked Gudrun, finally taking a sip of her drink now that she was somewhat calmer.

"I have. I rang him last night because he'd been worried about me getting caught in the storm and had left me some messages. He eventually apologised for not coming to stay but I didn't mention what Anna had said."

"What are you going to do?"

"I don't know, I might have to leave it until I get home. It's not the kind of thing we can discuss on the phone."

"But what about you and Jonas?"

"There isn't a me and Jonas. I do like him and if I didn't have Adam, who knows? But I can't just break up with Adam after two years because of someone I've known for two minutes." If she was being truthful, Rachel more than liked Jonas but knowing that there was something special between them was making the decisions she had to make for her and Adam's future all the more difficult. It seemed more important than ever to make the right decision regardless of her feelings for Jonas.

"But what if he's The One? Can you take the risk? There aren't endless chances for love, Rachel. If you see it, you have to take the chance and if it is Jonas and not Adam, well maybe that's destiny."

Rachel had never believed in destiny. She hadn't believed in the notion of a soulmate. When she met Adam, they got along well, fitted easily into each other's lives, understood each other's work and yes, she thought that was love. Being with Jonas was different. From the way she tingled at his touch to the way her head had filled with stars when he kissed her, even if it was just on the cheek. That physical desire had never been there between her and Adam. They had good sex but she had never had that carnal urge to rip his clothes off and pin him down, covering him with hard, passionate kisses like she wanted to do to Jonas.

So, was Gudrun right? Should she give up a chance at what might be her one big love for the sake of loyalty to someone who now, she wasn't even sure was being loyal to her. Perhaps it was worth getting to the bottom of things with Adam before she went home after all.

Rachel and Gudrun spent the rest of the day running errands in the van that Nick had hired so that he and the build team could easily pick up anything they needed in the way of materials.

They went to IKEA and ordered the biggest sofa they could find, slouchy and inviting with deep seats and a dark grey cover which should make the display of cushions 'pop'. They also bought a low coffee table and a lovely kitchen island with a butcher's block top and two stainless steel shelves underneath which would be great for extra display space along with a couple of wooden bar stools to complete the look.

After that, they visited all of the places where they had left leaflets the previous week to see how many had been picked up. They began at Te & Kaffi, just a couple of doors away from Snug, went to the bookshop on the corner then headed for the wool shop.

As soon as they walked in and the lady behind the counter saw Rachel's hat, she smiled.

"Your hat looks wonderful!"

"Thank you, I really enjoyed knitting it."

In fact, she had missed knitting since she'd finished it and had thought that maybe she would knit another one as a present for someone.

"I'm glad you enjoyed it and I love the Pom-Pom. Hello Gudrun, how are you?" She came out from behind the counter and kissed Gudrun.

"This is Olafur's aunt, Katrin. Katrin, I guess you have met Rachel?"

"Yes, but I didn't know that she was from your shop."

Gudrun rolled her eyes at Rachel. "It's not my shop."

"So, you must be the girl who stayed in my cabin with Jonas on Saturday night?"

Rachel blushed right to her toes. "Yes, thank you so much for letting us stay."

"Oh, no," she waved away the thanks with her hand, "Jonas is one of the family, we were happy to help."

"Katrin, we were wondering whether we could leave some more leaflets for the Sung store with you? It looks like they've all gone," said Gudrun, waving a fan of leaflets in her hand.

"Oh, yes, do leave some more. A couple of people that took them will be just right for you. My friend's daughter weaves beautiful woollen blankets, she is planning to bring them to show you. She has just started so she hasn't got anywhere to sell them yet."

"Perfect, that's just the sort of thing we're looking for. We haven't got anything else like that at the moment."

Rachel was hoping that this would happen, that people would spread the word and they would find some beautiful things that weren't already available anywhere else in Reykjavik, or even Iceland if they were lucky.

That evening Rachel ate at the Noodle Bar before she went back to the hotel. She'd had a brilliant day because as well as running errands, she had been through her schedule with Gudrun. They'd tweaked the timings of some things, added in a couple of trips to designers and talked endlessly about merchandising; the thing they were both looking forward to the most.

Rachel had missed a call from her mum at just after 6 pm. Her parents were of the generation who would always wait until after 6 pm to make a call because they still thought it was cheaper. Rachel was pretty sure it didn't make any difference these days.

"Hi Mum!" Rachel sat on the bed staring at the two carrier bags of wool knowing that's why her mum had rung, sounding more jovial than she felt.

"Rachel! I tried to ring you earlier, isn't that funny?"

Her mum had only just got to grips with owning a mobile phone and was not au fait with any of the functions, like missed calls.

"I saw on my phone that you'd tried to ring, Mum. How are you both?"

"Well, Dad put his back out digging up the ornamental cherry so goodness knows when we'll be able to move that now. It needs doing before it starts to bud."

It was typical of her to worry more about moving the tree than her husband's back injury.

"Is he alright?"

"Yes, he's fine now but he won't be able to do any jobs in the garden for a couple of weeks."

That would be so irritating for her mum who wanted everything to happen immediately. Which made Rachel think she rang because...

"Anyway, I rang to see whether Adam could post the wool to me. I know I said it would wait until I see you but Sylvia is getting impatient so I thought that would be easier if he doesn't mind."

Here we go, thought Rachel.

"Sorry Mum but it's still here."

"Oh, he didn't have room for it?" She sounded disappointed.

Rachel tensed, bracing herself for the change to disapproval.

"No, he didn't come over in the end. He had to work over the weekend to finalise a deal he'd been working on."

"Oh, Rachel."

Tears sprang to her eyes because her mum sounded sympathetic and sorry for her. It made her feel homesick and she had a fleeting feeling of wanting to be looked after by her mum, for her to make it all better.

"It's fine. I'm fine. He was really sorry, he couldn't do anything about it."

"Oh, love. It's such a shame for you. Your dad and I do worry about you."

"Thanks, Mum. I'm okay. I had a lovely weekend anyway. I went on a sightseeing tour."

Even though Rachel was just saying it to reassure her mother, she actually *had* had a lovely weekend.

"Well, that's good love. We just want you to be happy and we do like Adam, we just worry when he lets you down. You deserve better than that."

Rachel's mother was rarely so frank. Yes, she did make disapproving noises, probably without realising it, so Rachel knew what she thought, but she'd never said it out loud.

After further reassurances from Rachel that she was alright and after her mother had regaled her with tales of the latest Skype call from her brother, she said goodbye and settled into bed with her new knitting.

Now that she was more practised with her knitting, Rachel found that it lulled her into a very relaxed state which allowed her mind to wander, a bit like when she was swimming. Whether that was a good thing at the moment, she didn't know.

Nothing felt like real life. The things she had seen here were so otherworldly and the climate and the strange dusk that enveloped much of the day added to that feeling. Being trapped in a snowstorm with a handsome, protective man in a magical foreign land was at the top of the list of reasons why it didn't feel like real life. Looking back on that night in particular made Rachel feel like Cinderella after the ball; she'd had a wonderful night but it could never be.

Jonas was the polar opposite of Adam; a free spirit to Adam's calculated planning; spontaneous, fun-loving and relaxed as opposed to Adam's more reserved, well-groomed ways. Allowing her mind to wander, Rachel thought about how Jonas made her melt when he looked at her sometimes. He just caught her eye fleetingly with a look that took her breath away with its intensity. She knew he felt something for her too. There was no denying that they were falling for each other and being so removed from her usual life gave Rachel a perspective that she hadn't had before. She could see how her life would be if she went back to London, even now, before anything really had happened between her and Jonas and that wasn't the life she wanted anymore. This was an opportunity she needed to take. After all, wasn't that what had brought her to Iceland in the first place? Taking one opportunity and going back to normal afterwards wasn't going to work. She was on a trajectory out of her life in London and that was where she wanted to stay.

21

The store was starting to take shape now. The interior walls had been painted and the ceiling was up. The windows flooded the space with natural light and as soon as the floor covering was removed they would see how it all came together.

Because of the floor problem delaying everything, it had been decided that they'd concentrate all the efforts of Nick and his team on the main shop floor and not worry about having the downstairs office and stock room completely finished for the opening. Although Rachel had gone along with it at the time, she was aware that as soon as the stock started to arrive they would need to fill the stock room with any excess. Luisa was all for leaving it as it stood and just cleaning it up but Rachel thought it needed a bit more than that to keep the stock clean and fresh smelling. Despite it being her and Gudrun's day off, she decided to devote a day to it herself. It didn't matter to anyone what the standard of finish was like because no-one would notice once it was full of stock.

Rachel dragged Nick away from something he was doing with the wall lights and took him downstairs to find out what she would need to buy to paint and freshen up the stockroom.

"We'll have time to do that before we go, you don't want to get into it do you?" He stood there with his arms crossed, looking at her with an amused smile.

"Even if you were going to have time, it'll be too late by then because the stock will be here and it needs to go somewhere. As soon as this room's full, there won't be another opportunity. I don't mind, it'll only take a day to slap some paint on."

"Well, okay then," he said with a tone that sounded like 'I told you so'. "You'll need a couple of litres of white emulsion and I'd get a couple of litres of floor paint to cover that concrete so it'll stop the dust and be easier to sweep over. You'll probably want to fill the cracks between the ceiling and walls with some Polyfilla and put some in those holes from the shelving that was here before otherwise, you'll get brick dust in the paint as soon as you start."

It sounded like quite a lot of stuff to do in one day, but Rachel was undaunted.

"Brilliant, thanks. Where's the best place to go for that then?"

"We've got an account at a builders' merchants, it's just off the motorway as you head out of town in the direction of the airport. You sure you want to?" She nodded. "I'd get a couple of rollers and trays as well."

He turned and headed back upstairs, shaking his head as he went. Admittedly Rachel had never done any DIY before but he didn't know that. She might turn out to be a brilliant decorator and it was just a stock room after all.

The builders' merchants was fairly easy to find but Rachel found it slightly less easy to find what she needed once she got there. Not knowing what Polyfilla was presented a bit of a problem but as usual, the impeccable English-speaking Icelanders easily bridged the gap between her very limited knowledge of what she needed and her ability to explain it to them. The temptation to choose some paint other than white was immense with her instinct telling her to choose mustard to go with the dull grey concrete floor paint but she thought that Nick would think that was a step too far and she'd never seen a stockroom painted anything but white so maybe there was a good reason for that.

As Rachel was signing the paperwork to get it charged to the Snug account, she heard a familiar voice. Jonas was talking to another member of staff on the opposite side of the counter. He had his back to her so she assumed he hadn't seen her and she could easily have left without having to encounter him at all but now that a few days had passed since the snowstorm, she wanted to see him.

She loaded up her various cans and decorating paraphernalia onto her trolley and then with her heart pounding, she called over to him.

"Hey, Jonas!"

He turned around and smiled when he saw her, said something in Icelandic to the guy he was talking to, they shook hands and he came over and kissed her on the cheek, looking pleased to see her. Rachel had turned into a grinning idiot, equally pleased to see him and finding the combination of the kiss and his sparkly eyes mesmerising.

"Rachel! It is good to see you. I hope you're not decorating that shop on your own," he joked.

"Just the stockroom, we haven't got time to have it done properly so I thought I'd have a go. What are you doing here?"

He didn't have any shopping and Rachel thought he probably spent too much time outdoors to be bothered about home improvements anyway.

"I came to see Gunnar, he does some guide work for me sometimes. He leads that glacier walk which we went on."

"Oh, cool."

Rachel longed to be back on that walk, just at the moment Jonas took her in his arms as he saved her from the sheer drop…although she was romanticising now because she knew at the time she had been a nervous wreck and only had a fleeting memory of Jonas grabbing her.

"Can I help you take that back to the shop?"

She didn't need any help but she didn't want him to go either.

"If you could give me hand to get it in the van that would be great, thanks."

He took the trolley from her and pushed it out to the car park. It was lucky he had helped because there was a lot of compacted snow which required quite a lot of heaving to manoeuvre the trolley over, even for Jonas. They put the shopping in the back of the van and stood with the trolley between them.

"It was really nice to see you," said Rachel, hoping that Jonas would tell by her eyes how much she meant it.

"It was nice to see you too," he said gently. Then he looked up to the sky and exhaled, puffing his cheeks out. "I like you, Rachel." He paused to look at her before carrying on. "I think you like me too and I know it's complicated but I had to tell you."

"I feel the same way," Rachel blurted out before she could think better of it. "But yes, it is complicated and I…"

"It's okay," said Jonas gently as he took her hand and squeezed it. "I know you can't…I know. But I can't stop thinking about you and I had to tell you in case there was any chance."

He looked so serious. No-one had ever laid their out their feelings to her so openly before and she took it as a sign.

There is a chance, she wanted to say but with her life feeling like it was in limbo, it was wrong to give him hope. "I do feel the same, Jonas. It's just so…complicated." That was the only word she could think of to sum up how she was feeling.

"Well, you know where to find me. I would love to see you again." He pulled her towards him into a brief embrace before he kissed her quickly on the lips and walked away without looking back.

All the way back to the shop Rachel was thinking about what Jonas had said. It had opened up an almost overwhelming feeling inside her. She wanted to throw herself into his arms and have him hold her and kiss her. Properly. Now she knew he felt the same way as her, that the chemistry between them, he felt too, it had helped her make her mind up. She had to speak to Adam. She'd Skype him which was at least slightly better than a phone call.

Rachel cracked open the paint and began painting, working from the top down which was about the only decorating rule she knew about. There was no refinement in her technique at all, she was just slapping the paint on to get the job done as quickly as she could.

At lunchtime, she popped to the bakery across the road and picked up some sandwiches and cakes for the team. It was cold, though thankfully the heating system in the shop had been commissioned and was working just fine. Nick and Rachel sat perched on the counter and surveyed the store, pointing things out to each other between mouthfuls. It was snagging time, which meant looking around the store picking up small bits and pieces that needed sorting out before it would be finished. Rachel had a couple of issues with the placement of some of the shelving and wanted to move it around which meant she needed to speak to Luisa so that she was aware of the changes. Nick wanted to change the positioning of the counter unit because it was proving difficult to wire the data connection for the till where they had decided to place it. None of the snagging items were major issues but they needed to make sure everything was picked up over the next two or three days.

Luisa picked up the Skype call as soon as Rachel had launched it and it wasn't until she saw herself in the camera that she realised she had paint splattered in her hair.

"I hope the store is looking tidier than you, Rachel."

Rachel tousled her fringe as if that would instantly improve her appearance but in fact, it just made her hair stick out at all angles instead.

"Hi, Luisa! Yes, it is. I've just been slapping some paint on the stockroom walls."

"Nice to see you getting stuck into it. Still on schedule?"

"Yes, we've just started snagging. There are a couple of shelves that could do with moving. I was going to mark them on the drawing and send that over for you to see. Also, Nick will need to move the counter position because of a problem with getting the data connection. I can mark that too but I'm not sure yet how much of a move it needs. He's going to sort that out first so I can let you know how it goes."

"Remember that the flow of the store needs to be preserved above everything else. If the counter moves too far... Well, I'll leave it to you. You know the issues with it."

"Hopefully, moving the other shelves I mentioned will improve the flow in the back -left corner because it was going to be a bit of a dead zone. That might alleviate any problem with moving the counter anyway."

At this stage, you could have the most perfect layout drawing but until you saw it all built and could see how the display areas were going to work once you'd merchandised the store, you couldn't tell whether it was going to work as you'd planned on paper.

"I trust your judgement, Rachel. That's what you're there for. Did you get the info about the freight?"

"Yes, we'll be ready for it. Gudrun's been brilliant, she's a real asset. We've been out meeting designers too so we're both hopeful that there will be some fantastic new stock for you to see."

"That sounds brilliant. It's been worth having Gudrun on board early then so we're not totally relying on the Design Call."

"Definitely. I can't wait for you to see some of the things we've found. Okay, well barring any other issues, I'll see you next week."

"Great. Oh, and can you drop me an email to let me know when the freight arrives? We paid for the expedited service and I want to make sure we get it. Thanks Rachel," she said, ending the call.

Before Rachel started painting again, she tried to establish with Nick where the counter was going to end up. At the moment, it was on the right -hand side of the shop, running parallel to the sidewall about halfway down. Nick wanted to shift it a metre nearer to the back of the store and even with her shelf shuffling at the back she would have to do something else to keep the flow intact.

These last-minute problems were what Rachel thrived on and this was the first time she had been sorting it out on-site rather than liaising from the office because usually, Luisa was the one in this position, albeit probably not painting.

Her slapdash painting efforts were just about finished when Nick yelled from upstairs. "Rachel, come and check this is all okay then!"

They'd moved the shelves and the counter around with everything now still needing to be made good and fixed back properly. Rachel didn't love the new counter position; it was too far towards the back of the store and had looked better where it was before but it was workable. They couldn't live without the data connection for the till so there wasn't a lot of choice and it was very rare that they opened a store without deviating from the original plans in some way or another.

All of these things were still running through Rachel's mind when she locked the shop up that evening. She had decided to go swimming, grab a hot dog at the pool and then go back to the hotel to mark up the drawings to send to Luisa. But before that, she had to go back to the hotel for a shower before her swim because she couldn't very well turn up with paint all over her.

Less than an hour later she had done a few lengths of the pool to make herself feel that she deserved the soak she was having in the hot saltwater pool, surrounded by snow. The sky was cloudy but there were clear patches for a few minutes at a time so Rachel lay with her head just out of the water, looking at the stars and, as usual, hoping against all probability for a glimpse of the Northern Lights. Her mind had stopped going over the next couple of days work at the shop and had been filled instead with thoughts of Adam.

She had a churning feeling in her chest whenever she thought of him because of the unresolved business of whether or not Anna had seen him out with someone else. The problem was that ever since she had decided she needed to confront him about it, she had been trying to play out how the conversation would go between them but given that there were infinite outcomes, she ended up unable to predict what might be said. Rachel really preferred to be on much more solid ground than that, which had led her to this limbo. But enough was enough. She was a strong person, stronger in Iceland somehow than she felt at home and finally, she felt ready.

Once she got back to the hotel, with the churning feeling threatening to turn into something a little messier, she sat on the bed with the laptop in front of her and called Adam. It began to ring. Every ring seemed to last an eternity and she wanted to hang up but wished Adam would answer all at the same time.

"Hi Rach," he said as his face filled the screen.

He looked pretty wretched which surprised her.

"I'm so sorry about the weekend. I don't know what to say."

"I can't believe you didn't come. I really thought you would."

"Rach, I wanted to. Believe me, I couldn't get away. It was just bad timing. I had said I might not make it."

He hadn't. If he'd said that, she would have known for sure that he wasn't going to come because it wouldn't have been the first time that he'd laid the groundwork to let her down.

"Adam, you didn't say that to me. I thought it was different this time, that you really wanted to come."

"Sorry. I know it's no excuse but I thought you knew it wasn't a firm arrangement." He looked surprised which made Rachel's blood boil.

"A firm arrangement? It wasn't a business meeting, Adam. It was supposed to be special, time for us to be together. When was the last time that happened? Of course it was a firm arrangement."

She paused for what seemed like ages and Adam didn't say anything. Perhaps he was trying to think of the last time they'd done anything out of the ordinary together. Good luck to him because aside from the Icebar, she had struggled.

"It's over," she said.

In that moment, she was so certain that she couldn't believe she had waited so long to put an end to it. No one should have to put up with being in a relationship where they were constantly let down and overlooked. That wasn't love. Rachel knew that now. Now that she'd had a chance to be away from the grind of her normal life.

She could breathe here, see what mattered, allow *herself* to be what mattered for a change.

"What?"

She could see the scorn on his face. "It's over, Adam."

"I heard what you said. What the hell are you talking about? Are you seriously ending it because I didn't come on holiday with you?"

Even now he thought it was about that. He saw everything in isolation whether it was work or their relationship and Rachel had come to realise that was always going to be the case. He didn't see how lots of small disappointments could mount up and become the precipice that their relationship was teetering on the edge of.

"It's not just about this. It's the latest in a long list of times when I haven't been your top priority and this time it really mattered. I can't be an afterthought. I deserve more than that. And I deserve more than finding out you've been seeing someone else while I've been away."

Even over Skype, Rachel could see him turn pale and she held her breath waiting for his response.

"I don't know what you mean," he began, "I would never cheat on you, Rach."

"Anna called and said she saw you with someone in that new bar off Seven Dials."

"It was just someone from work. It was just a kiss, Rach, that's all, I was drunk. It didn't mean anything."

But it meant everything. It meant that all the times he'd been late home he could have been with someone else. It was just a kiss *this* time.

At that moment, once she knew that what Anna had seen was more than harmless flirting, her overriding reason for breaking up with him was that he was a cheat because she knew that wasn't something she could ever get over.

"That's it, Adam. It *is* over. It's not just because you didn't come over, it was lots of things but now it's because you cheated on me."

"A kiss isn't cheating! It was a mistake and it was the first and last time, I promise."

"Do you know what? I don't need this. I deserve to be with someone who thinks I'm worth being with. Not someone who's there if they've got nothing else to do. I need someone I can depend on and it's not you, Adam. I couldn't see it before but now…"

"You can't do it like this, Rach, it's not fair. Wait until you come home and we'll talk about it. Once you get home you'll feel differently, get some perspective back…"

"I have plenty of perspective and it took being away for me to get it."

"Rach, that's so unfair," he whined. "You love working hard just as much as I do. You know that's why I couldn't come. I tied up the Scramble deal on the Saturday when I would have been in Iceland. What should I have done? If I'd come, I'd have been walking away from that bonus that's taken a year of hard work."

"Other people manage to have time off, Adam. This was a long-standing arrangement and it was just a weekend. The deal could have happened on Friday or Monday if you'd wanted it to. You let your job dictate your whole life and that means it dictates mine too and it's not fair."

"Look, Rach, Jim has asked me to go into business with him and I'm going to hand in my notice at Grainger Jones. Things can be better between us. I can be my own boss and things will be different, I promise."

"It won't make any difference because no one tells you to be like this, it's all you. Being your own boss won't change anything as far as our relationship goes." She knew she was right. If anything, he'd be working even more hours if he was trying to launch a new business.

"Whatever you're feeling now it's not real, being away has made you forget how great things were between us before you left."

"I would have said that too but now all I remember is me waiting at home for you to come in, then instead getting a late-night call or sometimes only a text to say you were going to stay in town, apparently with clients but who knows? I realise now I had no idea what was going on."

He had his head in his hands and didn't attempt to tell her she was wrong. That told her everything.

"The past three weeks have shown me there's more to life than work and it's shown me a different side to you. There are amazing things out there that we never make time to see and being together and seeing them, that's what life's about. I wanted to show you that at the weekend but you're not going to be that person, Adam. I don't think you *can* be and I knew that when you didn't come."

"So, it was some sort of test and I failed it," he said bitterly.

"No, it wasn't. But everything made sense and I'm so sorry to be doing it like this, so sorry, Adam, but I have to. I can't wait until I get home. I love you but really, I mean it. It's over," she said gently.

His eyes had been lowered while she was talking and now he looked into the camera again, she could see that they were full of tears. They sat in silence for what felt like minutes because there was nothing else to say. Rachel ended the call and shut down her laptop.

She lay back on the bed and a sob engulfed her. She pressed her hands to her face, trying to muffle the wail that she could hear was coming from her but she was powerless to stop. The relief she'd known would come was there, and she clung to its frail presence as she grieved for her and Adam. It was almost a physical pain, overwhelming but cathartic at the same time.

22

Rachel spent the next day arranging and labelling the stockroom shelving, tidying and cable-tying all the cables for the computers, till and phones and building the IKEA furniture so that it was together before Nick left the following day just in case she needed help with anything before he left. She'd also started sticking the corporate vinyl on the walls, a job which she looked forward to but which gave her palpitations in case she got a bubble underneath.

Though it was her day off, Gudrun arrived at 6 pm just as it was starting to look almost finished and she, Rachel and Nick walked around every inch of the store making a final list of things that needed to be done before he left. There was hardly anything. Everything was just where it should be and it left Rachel feeling positive that they were going to be delivering a great Snug store next week.

"Do you want to get dinner, Rachel?" asked Gudrun as they locked the shop.

"I'd love to. I'm starving actually, where shall we go?"

"How about Islenski Barinn?"

"Perfect. I could do with a drink, to be honest."

"You can't have had a bad day, Rachel. Everything looks great!"

"I broke up with Adam last night."

Gudrun put her hand over her mouth and gasped, wide-eyed. "You did not! *Guð minn góður*! How did it go?"

"It was horrible but I did end up feeling relieved," explained Rachel as they strolled up the road past the fairy-lit trees. "He wasn't expecting it, but the conversation just fizzled to nothing in the end. He thought it was purely because he didn't come over last weekend. He didn't seem to understand that it was about everything, not just that. Or I didn't explain properly."

"Did you confront him about the other woman?"

Rachel nodded.

"And he denied it?"

"Actually no. He assumed Anna had seen more than she did and he admitted he'd kissed this woman. He said it was a mistake and that it was the first time it had happened."

Gudrun snorted in disbelief. "He would say that."

"I know. I kind of doubt it was the first time or that it stopped at kissing and it did end up being more about that than the fact that he didn't come for the weekend. I don't think he realised it would matter to me. I've probably let things like that go before without much fuss but it was the straw that broke the camel's back."

While Gudrun looked confused at the English metaphor, Rachel had a sudden pang of guilt. Had he understood her reasons properly and had she given him a chance to explain his side of things? Not that anything he said would have made any difference. It was a big decision she'd made and if it was the right decision nothing should have been able to change her mind. No doubt there would be more talking when she got home. In the meantime, she just hoped he'd be able to accept it.

Gudrun was such good company that Rachel managed to have a great evening. They inevitably talked about men with Gudrun imparting advice about the break-up.

"The thing is Rachel, you need to move on. You are the one who made the decision and it was a good decision. Time is short," she added, giving Rachel a knowing look as she sipped her wine.

"I know you think I should be straight round to Jonas's," smiled Rachel, "but that wasn't why I broke up with Adam."

"No, you broke up with him because he didn't realise how lucky he was and because you deserve someone who does realise."

"Exactly. But it was two years and I did love him. I was just blinkered to the wider world beyond London and work. I thought if Adam came here he would see things the same way as me but I don't think that would ever have happened. He works because that's what he loves, it's his life. In London, I did work almost as much as him but in hindsight, it was a time filler. I love working for Snug but if Adam had been around more we would have spent more time together and both of us might have had a life outside of work. I know now that's what I want."

"Skál!" said Gudrun, holding her glass up to be clinked.

"Skál!" Rachel replied, feeling as if this was the first night of the rest of her life.

*

The next day, Rachel and Gudrun set off to visit another designer, a potter who used lava in his work to produce something which was certainly very unique although Rachel wasn't entirely sure she was in love with the outcome. It was sometimes good to meet the artist and see where they worked to help put the work into context, so she was trying to keep an open mind.

They were just parking up when Rachel's phone rang, showing the number from Jonas's excursion company.

"It's Jonas, I think."

"I'll meet you inside," said Gudrun, pulling on the handbrake and then getting out and putting her coat on.

"Hello?" said Rachel.

"Hi, Rachel. It's Jonas. How are you? I hope you don't mind me calling you."

"No, it's fine. What can I do for you?" Rachel could see Gudrun watching as she loitered over by the door of the studio, turning away when she saw Rachel looking.

"I wondered if you'd like to go out for a drink tonight?"

Judging by Gudrun's behaviour, Rachel guessed that news of her break-up with Adam had reached Jonas via Olafur. At least she could say yes with a clear conscience with no need to bother justifying it to herself.

"That would be great. Where shall I meet you?"

"I'll come to the hotel for you. Is 8.30 okay?" Ever the gentleman.

"Perfect. See you later."

Rachel walked over to where Gudrun was grinning like a loon.

"So, was that Jonas?" she asked.

"You know it was. I assume he's heard about me and Adam?"

"Who knows?" said Gudrun, attempting an expression of innocence before she turned and went inside.

*

At just before 8.30 pm Rachel went downstairs and waited inside the hotel lobby for Jonas. Right on time he came around the corner, grinned at her and kissed her on the cheek once she'd skipped down the steps to meet him. His affectionate greetings made her feel really special. And he was never late.

"Ready?" he asked, taking her mittened hand.

"Yes, lead the way."

Rachel had guessed they might go to Islenski Barinn but instead of turning up towards Laugavegur, they carried on towards the harbour. Aside from visiting the Harpa, Rachel hadn't ventured around that part of town at all, assuming that all there was to see were fishing boats and buildings to do with fishing and that is exactly how it looked to her now.

"Really?" She looked at Jonas with her eyebrows raised, seriously doubting that there could be anywhere in this area to find a drink.

"Really. Have you not realised yet that I know all the best places to go?"

He squeezed her hand and they carried on, walking on the quayside, towards the black of the sea, between the boats and the buildings. The sky was clear and the moon was almost full so they could easily see where they were going; right to the end of the quay by the looks of it.

As they reached the corner where the quayside turned to the left, Rachel could see that there was a building with lights on, the only one. It looked like all the other buildings on the quay in that it was white, tall but single-storey with just a few small windows fairly high up. She guessed that it must have been a warehouse or something similar. Whatever it was now, the exterior wasn't giving anything away. The doorway was lit by two storm lanterns hung either side. Jonas held the door open for her and she stepped into the warmth.

The whole place seemed to be lit almost entirely by fairy lights with storm lanterns hanging in between. It was very atmospheric and cosy. There was a wide balcony, like a mezzanine level, running around three walls which made the underneath very intimate and the only wall which had the full height of the building was where the bar was. It ran the full width of the building and had shelves which no-one could possibly reach, right up to the ceiling, full of bottles of clear liquid. It was beyond cool; the shelves were lit with colour-changing lights so that the bottles seemed to be full of colour-changing liquid.

They found a table, a booth really, with wooden high back benches which had reindeer skin throws over the seats. Rachel found that a bit disconcerting but Jonas explained that they were a by-product of the meat industry in other Scandinavian countries.

The bar was dedicated to gin and tonic and offered a huge range. Rachel had no idea what to choose so she left it to Jonas. Her drink ended up being a gin and tonic, obviously, with some pink ice cubes that gradually turned the drink pink and subtly enhanced the flavour.

"This place is cool, those shelves behind the bar look amazing," she said, once Jonas had sat down opposite her.

"One of my friends opened it about six months ago. His family used to fish and owned this building but now they land the fish in a more modern port north of the city so the building wasn't needed any more."

After a minute, he reached for her hand across the table and looked at her very seriously.

"Jonas," she began.

"No, Rachel," he said softly. "Don't say anything. I know you have split up with your partner and I'm sorry about that. It must have been difficult for you. I think you know how I feel about you and I think you feel the same. I'm not asking you to choose me forever but for tonight at least and as many days as we can get. Thinking about what would happen when you leave will just spoil the time we have now. Let's just accept that we like each other and enjoy being with each other and there's nothing wrong with that if it makes us happy."

He made it sound so straightforward. Maybe it *was* straightforward.

"Well, I can't say it's not a good idea," Rachel said, smiling at him as she looked into his blue eyes that could not have looked more longing, "but it's not really 'me' to have a fling. It's like a holiday romance except I'm not on holiday."

"It's more than that for me," Jonas said softly.

"I was being flippant. I'm sorry. I do like you Jonas, I have from the first time we met and all the time we've spent together has been wonderful."

It felt so easy to be completely honest with him.

"But I'm scared about getting involved with you when I'm leaving next week." She was scared because she knew it would never be enough time. It ought to be because it was too soon after Adam to start something new but it didn't feel like something new. It felt like something that had been there all the time and the most natural thing in the world.

"It's completely up to you, Rachel and I understand if you say no, but I think if we both feel the same, we could explore whatever that is while we can and after that, well, let's worry about that later."

Jonas squeezed her hand again and went to get another round from the bar.

"Let's do it," she said when he came back. "If I've learned anything from coming here it's that life is out there and we should take every chance that comes our way."

He smiled and clinked his glass against hers.

"To us. For as long as we can have," he said.

Thinking about what might happen when it was time for her to go home was something that could wait until some other time.

"So, what will our next adventure be?" asked Jonas

"If by adventure you mean finding ourselves in mortal danger again, then count me out," Rachel said, trying to sound serious.

"Oh, come on! That was the real Iceland, not many tourists are lucky enough to have that experience. It will be the best story you tell when you get home."

"Well, I still haven't seen the Northern Lights," she pointed out.

"That's true. We have to see the aurora. Next time it is a clear night we will go. We could have gone tonight, except now," he said, gesturing to their drinks.

"Never mind. I'm sure there will be another chance."

"Yes, even in winter there is a good chance of clear sky more than once in two weeks," he said drily. "Let's drink to that, Skál!"

The rest of the evening was light-hearted and good fun. After another gin and tonic each, they wandered back to the hotel. Jonas, ever chivalrous, kissed Rachel on the cheek but she took both of his hands in hers and kissed him gently on the lips.

"Thank you for tonight," she whispered as they drew apart. He didn't say anything, just squeezed her hands and began to kiss her, properly. The pit of her stomach ached with longing and she kissed him more fiercely. His hand cupped the nape of her neck and gently drew her in closer if that was possible. Without saying anything to each other, a knowing look between them saying everything, they broke apart and still holding hands went into the hotel where she led him to her room.

They stood across the bed from each other, looking with intent and desire at one another as they peeled their various layers of clothing off in silence. Jonas knelt on the bed and held his hand out, beckoning her towards him. It was the first time she'd seen him naked. She knew he was toned from seeing him in his thermals when they were snowed in together but he was lean and subtly muscular probably from being so active rather than from going to the gym.

As Rachel made her way onto the bed, he laid her down beneath him and started gently kissing her face, not her lips, working his way down with feather-light kisses across her breasts, down her stomach then back to her breasts, teasing her until she had her fingers in his hair trying to bring his mouth to hers but he resisted and all she got were more kisses on her cheek. She nuzzled into his neck, arching herself towards him, feeling the hardness of him for the first time. He put his hands on her hips and took his kisses downwards, sending her to somewhere she hadn't been for the longest time. She could feel the beautiful wave of pleasure starting to surge within her. At just the right moment, he slid upwards, filling her with the warmth and firmness that her body craved. They clung to each other, urgently pressing together as if they weren't close enough, moving together as if they had made love a hundred times before and reaching the pinnacle at exactly the same moment.

It was complete perfection.

But it had also made everything a while lot harder for both of them.

23

Rachel woke to find Jonas lying on his side watching her.

"What are you doing?" she asked sleepily.

"I'm watching you sleep," he smiled. "Not really, that sounds *skrýtið*."

"I hope that means weird," she said, turning to face him.

He grinned, telling her that she was right. "I was waiting for you to wake up," he said. "Are you free today? I have an idea."

He was so much perkier than she felt.

"What time is it?" She snuggled further under the duvet and wished he would do the same.

"Rachel..." He stroked her cheek with his fingers and then gently lifted one of her eyelids.

"Jonas! Okay, I'm awake."

He pulled her into him. "Sorry, but it is going to be a beautiful day. Let's make the most of it. Can you have the day off?"

"I probably could. I'll see if it's okay with Gudrun."

Jonas passed her phone from the bedside table and she typed off a quick text to Gudrun.

She leant over Jonas's chest to put her phone back, now that she was awake, suddenly aware that they were both naked, in bed together. It felt like it had been a long time coming and it felt right. "I love this," she said, resting her head on his chest.

"So do I."

They lay for a few minutes in silence until Rachel's phone pinged with a text from Gudrun confirming that she was going to be more than okay and that she was thrilled Rachel was taking the day off to be with Jonas.

"Okay, I'm all yours. What's the plan?"

"It's a secret but you'll love it."

Rachel snuggled further under the covers. "We could stay in bed for a bit," she said, kissing Jonas's neck.

"We could." He pulled away and by the mischievous look in his eyes Rachel could tell she'd won him over and managed to put him off wanting to get out of bed.

"We're making things hard for ourselves," Rachel said as they lay said by side afterwards, holding hands.

"I think it is worth it." Jonas squeezed her hand.

"Me too." It was easy to ignore the fact that they had such a short amount of time when they were together like this and somehow, the thought of leaving Jonas behind was still not as bad as the thought that they might never have found each other in the first place.

"But we cannot stay in bed all the time." He threw off the covers and headed into the bathroom. "We have things to do." He grinned. "Get up."

Rachel groaned. "I'll get up when you've finished in there." She saw him roll his eyes just before he closed the door and it filled her with delight that he was here with her. She loved the feeling of total acceptance that they already had with one another. It was as if they fitted together perfectly and had hardly anything more they needed to know about each other and yet everything to still discover. It felt magical.

"Make sure you wear layers and bring your waterproofs and snow boots. Probably wear everything you have," he said when he came out of the bathroom.

"Where are we going? Because I don't have any proper waterproofs, just my normal coat and these trousers."

"That will be fine." He came over and gave her a gentle, lingering kiss. "You can borrow some of mine."

She was intrigued but nervous. Jonas was very outdoorsy and although she loved what she'd seen of Iceland so far, she knew there were a lot of much more adventurous things on offer that she really wouldn't be up for. She hoped Jonas realised that.

"So is it something like glacier walking, like a sightseeing thing?"

"It's a surprise. But we'll need to go to my house first so I can get changed." He was still wearing the jeans, shirt and jumper he'd been wearing the night before, of course.

Rachel was excited about seeing where he lived. It must be fairly close by because it had taken him no time at all to come to her rescue when she'd got locked in the shop. She wondered what it would be like.

Once she was ready, they left the hotel and walked towards Laugavegur. It was a clear, cold day.

"The weather is perfect today," said Jonas, taking her hand as soon as they had both put their gloves on. He looked at her and smiled, then leant in and kissed her. "I will not get tired of doing that."

No-one had ever looked at her the way he did. It was as if she could see everything he felt for her in his eyes. She kept looking up at him as they walked, each time he returned her smile with that look and she couldn't imagine ever getting tired of seeing it.

It only took about five minutes to get to Jonas's. It was on a small cobbled path somewhere uphill from the harbour but down from the church. His tiny garden was full of fairy lights and small stone statues.

"Are those gnomes?"

Jonas frowned. "I don't know what that is. These are trolls." They looked just like gnomes but unpainted, without hats and not as happy looking.

He led her up the front steps onto a tiny wooden veranda where a couple of chairs were piled with snow. Rachel wondered whether it was ever warm enough to sit out there, even in the summer.

The house was clad in dark red corrugated cladding and the roof was grey. It was small but smart looking. Jones opened the front door and led Rachel into a lounge which was the entire height of the building, reaching into the apex of the roof. Opposite the front door was a mezzanine level reached by a set of steep wooden stairs which were barely more than a glorified ladder.

"That's the bedroom," Jonas said, pointing to the mezzanine. "Bathroom and kitchen." He pointed to two doors underneath the bedroom. "I will just be a minute. Have a look around if you want." He kissed her then climbed the stairs to the bedroom.

The lounge had a two-seater sofa, an armchair and a pot-bellied wood-burning stove with a flue that reached right to the roof. Everything was comfortable looking, lived-in and quite neat.

Feeling like she was being too nosy but doing it anyway, Rachel headed into the kitchen. It was like something from an IKEA catalogue. Super tidy, minimalist and very cool. The window looked out onto someone else's garden, also strung with fairy lights. It was like living on the set of a Christmas film all year round but Rachel supposed it was dark so much of the time that it cheered people up.

"Okay." Jonas appeared behind her dressed in his usual outdoorsy clothes. He opened a cupboard which looked like a larder but which was full of an assortment of coats, trousers and various types of boots. "Let's take these," he said pulling out a huge coat and some over trousers which were lined with soft fleece. "You can use this coat if you like. This one will be warmer and it doesn't matter if it gets dirty."

"Oh God, why will it get dirty?" Her anxiety was building. All of the worst things Rachel could imagine suddenly seemed the most likely things that Jonas would choose for them to do.

"It probably won't, I just don't want you to spoil your coat."

"Okay, thanks," said Rachel, taking the coat and trousers from him uncertainly.

"You don't need to worry. You will enjoy this, it is not dangerous like the other things we have done." He smiled and dropped a kiss on her forehead as he wrapped his arms around her. She buried her head into his chest, breathed in his scent and felt calm. There was no need to worry about anything when she was with Jonas.

"Your house is gorgeous," she said, kissing him. "Shall we just stay here and have a lazy breakfast instead?"

"We can pick up some breakfast on the way. You're not still worried, are you? It's going to be fun."

He pulled away from her, grabbed a rucksack and a set of keys.

"Come on, let's go."

His jeep was parked a couple of streets away and had a good covering of snow over it. Jonas insisted Rachel wait inside while he swiped the snow off then he disappeared into a nearby bakery and emerged with coffee and a bag of something that Rachel hoped were pastries. She was starving.

"Shall we eat these now?" she asked.

"No, let's save them until we get there. It's not far."

They drove out of town on what Rachel thought was the same road as the one she took on the Golden Circle tour but as soon as they had emerged from the city and the snowy landscape lay in front of them for as far as they could see, Jonas pulled off onto a side track and parked outside a non-descript wooden-clad building.

"Here?"

He grinned and took the pastries and coffee from Rachel, before going ahead to unlock the door while she changed her coat for the one that he'd lent her.

She caught up with him and he held the door open for her. It was one huge space filled to the rafters with all kinds of outdoor equipment. There were endless loops of rope hanging from hooks on the walls and boards with hooks holding clamps and harnesses. There were racks of kayaks, diving equipment and even snowmobiles.

"Wow, this is amazing."

It was also freezing cold and as she followed Jonas through the piles of equipment she was glad to see him heading for a cosy-looking nook with a couple of old sofas surrounding a wood-burning stove. He took a box of matches and lit the kindling that was already there which immediately started to blaze in a way that made Rachel feel warmer just by looking at it.

"This is where we store all our equipment. A lot of it is only used in the summer so we have to keep it somewhere. Also, we come here for meetings if there are a lot of us because the office in town is too small."

Jonas put a couple of logs into the stove and then tore open the bag of pastries and laid it on the table, inviting Rachel to choose first.

"You do so many different things. Do you know how to do everything? Even diving?"

He smiled modestly and nodded. "This is all I've ever done. I have worked for excursion companies since I left school. It was the next step to start my own. You can mix your ideas with what you think people want and try to make it different from what the others are doing."

Rachel sipped her coffee. She admired Jonas for working hard to turn what he loved into a business, a successful business. And she admired him even more for still loving every minute of it. It would be easy to forget your passion in the pursuit of business success but as with the rest of his life, it seemed Jonas had the right balance.

"Have you ever ridden on a snowmobile?"

"Of course I haven't," she said, giving him a playful nudge. "I live in England. We get an inch of snow and the country grinds to a halt. I'm pretty sure the only people in England who have ever been on a snowmobile did it in another country."

"Okay. We'll ride together then. I'll drive to start but you can have a turn later on."

"Is it like riding a motorbike? Not that I've ever done that either."

"It'll be fine," said Jonas reassuringly. He took Rachel's coffee out of her hands and put it on the table. "You just need to relax."

He gently pushed her back so that she was lying in the corner of the sofa and he was looking down at her with that expression she loved, as if she were the only person in the world. Kissing him was not going to get old, she knew that. Every time they kissed it was like the first time and Rachel felt like time expanded as she got lost in those moments.

After a couple of minutes, he sat up and sighed. "I could stay here all day."

"Me too."

"We have to go."

"Do we?" She put a hand behind his head and pulled him back to her. One more kiss was all he would give in to though.

"We can't waste a beautiful day."

"I don't think we'd be wasting it."

"Come on, it will be worth the effort, I promise."

Rachel hauled herself off the sofa and finished her coffee as Jonas picked out several helmets for her to try until he was satisfied that she had the best fit. He opened a large door on the side of the building and pushed a snowmobile outside in readiness. He packed a bag into the cubby under the seat which had goodness knows what in it before locking everything up behind them.

He climbed onto the snowmobile and Rachel climbed on behind him. He half-turned his head. "Ready?" he asked, his voice muffled by his helmet.

"Ready!" she shouted.

He started the engine, gave it a couple of revs and they were off. Jonas started fairly slowly but once he speeded up Rachel was terrified that she would be thrown off the back of the snowmobile and hugged tightly to his back.

As ever, the scenery took her breath away. Being on the snowmobile instead of inside a vehicle made Rachel feel more connected with it. Despite the extra clothes and the helmet she wore, she could feel the cold and see everything more closely. They passed steaming pools of water which had broken through the ice and snow. Powder-like snow blew over them and she periodically had to take her hand and wipe her visor because once she'd relaxed, she was more worried about missing everything there was to see than she was about falling off.

They were traversing a proper wilderness. There were hardly any buildings save from the odd small isolated house or cabin and unless they happened to be near a road, no traffic and the roads they did see were quiet.

"We're almost there!" Jonas shouted, turning his head so that Rachel could hear him.

She squeezed him around his middle in reply. All she could make out was a small building, it looked like a shed from a distance but as they got closer she saw that it was next to a stream of water that was steaming and appeared to be warm enough that it had kept the snow off the rocks that edged it.

Jonas stopped the snowmobile and pulled off his helmet before he got off and then held out his hand to help Rachel.

"What do you think?"

It wasn't massively picturesque but as Rachel walked to the edge of the water, she could see how clear it was and when she pulled off her glove and dipped her hand in, it was easily as warm as the Blue Lagoon.

"It's lovely, like a natural Blue Lagoon."

"Shall we get in?"

Rachel thought he was joking but his face told her he wasn't. "But we didn't bring any swimming stuff."

Jonas shrugged and grinned. "What do we need? It is just us. I do have some towels." He pulled the bag out from under the snowmobile seat. "And we can leave our clothes in there," he said, pointing to the shed.

"You mean, skinny-dip?"

"That is exactly what I mean." He had a mischievous look on his face now. "Come on Rachel, this is proper Iceland. No-one comes on tours here, it's just for locals who know about it. You are very lucky."

He took her hand and led her to the shed. Inside it was still just a shed but had a wooden bench and hooks on the walls. Jonas started to undress, hanging his clothes on the hooks. Rachel wasn't sure what was holding her back. They'd seen each other naked, not in broad daylight like this, but still. It was just so funny to be faced with the thought of being completely naked out in the snow, in the middle of nowhere. She sighed and allowed the tension to fall away. This was exactly the kind of experience she should embrace and why she loved spending time with Jonas; you just never knew what was going to happen next.

Once they'd both undressed, Rachel wrapped herself in the towel that Jonas handed her although he had opted to carry his and stay completely starkers with no hint of shyness.

"We will need to be very quick across the snow. Follow me."

He darted out of the shed and sprinted across the snow to where there was a gap in the rocky edge and the water naturally ebbed onto the gravelly, volcanic ground.

Rachel couldn't help shrieking, it was so cold and her feet were grateful to be immersed in the shallow water while she stood and worked out her next move. Jonas had placed his towel on a rock next to the little beach and was already submerged in the water up to his neck with a dreamy look on his face.

"It's wonderful," he called.

Even over her feet it did feel wonderful. Rachel whipped off her towel, leaving it on top of Jonas's before she dipped herself down into the water which became much deeper where Jonas was. She'd never been skinny-dipping before but she could understand the appeal. It felt very freeing and was especially nice once she made her way over to him and they embraced, keeping themselves as submerged as they could all the time.

"This place is brilliant, Jonas. I was so worried that you'd make me go diving or climbing or something."

He kept his arm around her waist as he led them to an underwater rock which was positioned perfectly as a seat. "I think I know you would not enjoy that."

"Don't you think it's weird that you know that about me already?"

He shrugged. "It's not weird. I think it's a sign that we're right for each other."

It was true. The short time they'd been together hadn't really been spent getting to know each other because it felt like they already did.

"It's so right that I worry about what we're letting ourselves in for. When I leave."

But whatever she said, there was nothing she could do. She wanted to be with Jonas more than anything and whatever hurt she might be storing up for herself in the future, it somehow seemed worth it.

"We both understand the risks, agreed that we would enjoy being together for however long that is."

Rachel nodded. "I'm scared that won't be enough"

"Me too. But it is better than never having met at all and who knows what will happen?"

But Rachel couldn't imagine Jonas being anywhere else, certainly not London. Wasn't that why he'd split up with Hilde, because he couldn't leave his business? What else did he have? His life was inextricably linked to Iceland.

"I think we both know what will happen."

"I will be away for the next two nights after this one but when I get back we are going to spend every minute we can together. Every night for sure."

"Okay. But the opening isn't far away. I'll be really busy."

"We have time, Rachel. Let's enjoy it."

He was right. What was the point of dwelling over what was yet to happen, however inevitable it might feel? This minute, this day, that was all she needed to worry about and as with every other minute she spent with Jonas, it was perfect.

24

They'd said a sleepy goodbye to each other when Jonas left for work at some ridiculous hour that morning. As he was taking a three-day excursion to the south of the island they had made a vague plan to meet for dinner when he got back. Rachel had stayed in bed after he left, dozing, letting her mind wander.

It had been the most amazing couple of days. After they'd finished skinny-dipping Jonas had let her drive the snowmobile most of the way back to the storage shed then they'd driven back to town where he'd dropped his jeep off and they'd walked back to the hotel for another night of love-making.

Now, she was savouring the weariness of her body, a physical reminder of the day before and all she would have to keep her going until Jonas was back. Him going away was probably good timing though as today was a big day, the one Rachel had been looking forward to the most throughout the whole project. All the stock was arriving and she and Gudrun would spend the next two days filling the shelves, making displays and generally having a lot of fun.

Rachel arrived at the shop first and stood in the middle of the floor surveying the finished space. It was light, airy and would look brilliant once everything was in place. There was a knock at the door and Rachel opened it to find Gudrun on the doorstep, grinning, with coffees and pastries in her hands.

"Oooh, perfect!" Rachel said, taking them from her so that she could take her coat off. "I'm absolutely starving, I didn't have time for any breakfast this morning."

"Well, I am guessing it will be a long day for us. We will need plenty of energy."

They sat on the sofa in the window which was still covered by vinyl so that no-one could see in, and devoured their pastries.

"So, what's the plan?" said Gudrun, mid-mouthful.

"I've got a rough plan of where each product type needs to go which will be a starting point but we can change things around if we want to. Anything you think would work better somewhere else, just say. Shall we walk the store?" Rachel said, brushing the crumbs off her hands as she stood up.

It was retail speak for having a look round. As they did, Rachel answered Gudrun's questions about the placement of various things, some of which were different from the other stores she'd studied as part of her training. She took photos of everything and made copious notes which impressed Rachel no end.

They heard the delivery lorry arrive before anyone had banged on the door, it was so noisy compared to any of the other traffic that normally went past. They propped open the door of the shop and prepared to carry goodness knows how many boxes into the store. Everything was packed on huge pallets, taller than either Rachel or Gudrun and about a metre square at the base and there were around ten of them. Rachel had been expecting lots of individual cardboard boxes like they usually dealt with in the UK so she had to quickly revise her plan for unpacking. By the time all the pallets were unloaded and everything was in the store there was no floor space left to be seen. They collapsed onto the sofa and decided that they needed more coffee before they could even attempt to start unpacking the boxes.

They tried to identify what was in each box from the notations on the outside rather than having to open all of them as they went along. Once they knew which supplier it was from Rachel could tell which area of the shop it belonged to and they made piles of boxes according to that.

It was late afternoon before they had checked all the boxes and the shop looked like a bomb had hit it. There were piles of boxes everywhere and despite their attempt at organising as they went along, there were plenty of suppliers whose stock was split between different areas of the store so Rachel wasn't sure their careful organisation was going to help anyway. They picked their way through the boxes to the window sofa and slumped down, completely exhausted.

"I didn't expect there to be as much as this," said Gudrun with a sigh, all the excitement of the morning long gone. "Do you think we'll have room for everything?"

"It's definitely more than we would normally have but it will be more expensive to send lots of smaller amounts of stock over from the UK so I suppose they decided to send enough to see you through for a bit. At least if we have no response to the Design Call we won't have to worry about the shop looking empty."

They began unpacking boxes together so that Rachel could show Gudrun the tricks of how to arrange everything on the shelves, then Rachel took anything that should be in a different area over to where it should be and any spare stock down to the stock room. They took it in turns to do that in the end because Gudrun thought it would be a good idea if she knew where everything was down there.

Rachel's phone rang and seeing that it was Anna, she signalled to Gudrun to take a breather.

"Rachel Richards. When were you going to tell me?"

"About what?"

"About anything. You have left me to fend for myself and I don't know *anything* about what you're doing and I bet there's something because I know Adam was coming to stay and I know you went on a date with that bloke so, come on. Catch me up on everything."

"I am here to work, in case you had forgotten," Rachel said, smiling at Anna's outburst.

She glanced over at Gudrun and briefly thought that they'd get on like a house on fire if they ever met each other. Although whether Rachel could contend with both of them needing to know the ins and outs of everything...

"Work? I'm sorry? What's that? Haven't you been climbing mountains and stuff?"

Rachel spent the next few minutes explaining that she'd broken up with Adam and told Anna that she liked Jonas. All of this was interspersed with regular gasps from Anna.

"I just *knew* things were going on. I think I'm psychic," she said. "So how did Adam take it?"

"I don't know. Not great, I mean, it was awful but I haven't heard from him. He mentioned that he was leaving his job but it didn't occur to me to ask him about that given what I'd just done. But I am a bit worried about him. Do you think I should ring him?"

"Hmm. Maybe not. His ego's probably bruised so perhaps it's better to give him a bit of space. Weird though, that he'd leave his job."

"I know and I really can't believe that he would have done that without discussing it with me. Obviously, it should be his decision but it's a big deal to do that without telling your partner and I was still his partner then."

"Well, that just makes the decision to break up all the more right. I mean, he didn't come to visit you and hello? - gave you no notice. Someone else could have come instead."

"You, perhaps?" asked Rachel, grinning.

"Oh, that would have been a great idea," said Anna as if it had never occurred to her. "And he probably snogged someone else, don't forget."

"Yes, he actually did."

"He admitted it?"

"Yes, with not much prompting. I don't think he thought it was anything to be concerned about but there was more than just kissing anyway.

"Blimey, so, overall a good decision. And I assume you're seeing the Icelandic hunk now?"

"Yes, sort of although he's away for a few days."

"Go for it, Rach. Be happy."

"There's just not much time until I have to come home. It's going to be really hard, I wonder whether we've done the right thing."

"Oh God, you definitely have. Just enjoy yourself and don't worry so much about things that haven't happened yet.

"I keep telling myself that."

"I'm always right."

Telling Anna everything that had happened in the past week or so made Rachel realise that quite a lot *had* happened and given her a brief jolt into her real life away from Reykjavik. Being in London seemed like light years ago and she was finding the idea of going back hard to contemplate.

At 9 pm they called it a night, estimating that they had cleared about a third of the boxes and reasoning that they'd get more done after a good night's sleep. Rachel was exhausted but too hungry to turn Gudrun down when she suggested a quick bite to eat at Islenski Barinn. Gudrun was such good company and although they'd chatted all day about the merchandising and all manner of other things, they still talked easily together over some fish and chips in a basket with delicious tartare sauce and a beer at the pub.

"Are you and Jonas seeing each other again?" asked Gudrun with a twinkle in her eye.

"He's away for a couple of days but we're having dinner on Wednesday night."

"Olafur's gone on the trip too. Good timing with everything we have to do at the shop. Not so much for you and Jonas though. You probably want to spend every minute you can get together."

"Yes, I think our chances will be thin on the ground once everyone flies in from London for the Design Call and the launch."

"I'm so excited about the Design Call. So many of the postcards have been picked up, we should have lots of people. Will you sit in on it?"

"No, I think it will be you, Luisa and Julia. It's always brilliant to see what people turn up with, you'll love it."

"Anyway, back to business. Have you and Jonas talked about what will happen when you go back to London?"

"No. We just decided to enjoy whatever time we can get while I'm here, not that there's much time left now, and I'm trying not to think beyond that. I don't want to hurt him." And she didn't want to put herself in the position of being hurt.

"He knows how it is, Rachel. I think he's willing to take the risk from what Olafur says."

"But it's exactly the same situation that he was in before, with Hilde."

Gudrun shook her head vigorously. "No, it's nothing like that. In her mind, she had already left him long before she went to America. He was a little in denial but believe me, they were not happy and that is why she decided to leave."

"Oh right." Rachel wasn't sure if that made her feel better or not.

"Olafur thinks this is completely different, for you and Jonas."

"Do you two spend all your time talking about me and Jonas?"

"Yes, it is *all* we talk about. We like a good love story," she said looking into her glass to avoid Rachel's raised eyebrows.

"Well, it's hardly a love story. We've only just met."

"They all start somewhere, Rachel."

25

When Rachel arrived at the shop the next morning she could have sworn that there were twice as many boxes to unpack than they'd left the day before. Gudrun arrived shortly after her and came through the door groaning.

"I had eight hours sleep but I still feel like I only just left here," she said as they surveyed the work they still had to do.

"It'll be easier today and then the fun part will be tomorrow when we get to do the displays and things. It'll be worth all the shelf-stacking today. Promise!"

Rachel had had a text from Jonas early that morning checking that they were still on for dinner the following night. It made her feel all warm inside when she heard the notification and then saw his name on the screen. She'd texted back to say yes and had asked what they were doing that day on his excursion. He replied that they were climbing a volcano and visiting a black sand beach which had huge rocks of ice washed up on it. She was sorry she hadn't had time to see that. Maybe next time. And she felt sure that there would be a next time.

They worked hard but had fun at the same time. The boxes were starting to disappear and the store was taking shape; a lot of the shelves were full now and neither of them could wait until the next day when they could make it all look beautiful. Gudrun was desperate to arrange the cushions and candles in colour wheel order but Rachel was making sure that they had everything unpacked before anything like that happened. She knew it would be easy to get carried away on details so it was better to wait until nothing else needed doing.

At lunchtime, while she and Gudrun were lounging on the window sofa before they got back to work, Rachel rang Luisa to update her on how it was going and to get the final arrangements for the rest of the Snug team's visit for the opening.

"I'm glad it's going well, Rachel. I'll admit I was worried about how you'd cope with the delivery with it just being the two of you at the moment but it sounds like you'll be ready for us."

"Definitely. Do you know what flight you're getting on Friday? I can come and meet you all, it's not far to the airport from town."

"We're getting in early so that Julia will be in time for the Design Call. If you could organise the transfer for us, that would be great. Oh, by the way, Julia wanted a word. I'll just put you through. And, well done Rachel, I can't wait to see the store, and you, on Friday."

The phone beeped while Luisa transferred the call, then Julia, the Managing Director and the founder of Snug, came on the line.

"Hi Rachel, it's Julia. I hear from Luisa that everything is going smoothly?"

"Hi Julia, yes, it's looking great. We're looking forward to showing you on Friday."

"Look, I'm expecting a visit from a business consultant while we're over in Iceland. There's a chance they may arrive before us and may even call into the shop for a look around. Just to give you a heads-up. I'm not sure who they're going to send yet, but the company is called Finch Associates.

"No problem. I'll make them welcome."

"Great, and I'm sure I don't need to say that discretion is of the utmost importance. Thanks, Rachel." And she hung up.

Business consultant? What was that all about? And the request for discretion. It was highly odd. As far as she was aware, Rachel didn't think Snug had ever used outside consultants before and what would they be consulting about?

"Everything alright?" asked Gudrun from her prone position at the opposite end of the sofa.

"Mmm," Rachel said, still thinking about whether it was anything she needed to worry about. It was probably best forgotten and would all come out in the end when they met this consultant.

"I need to book a taxi to pick them all up from the airport on

Friday." Her phone beeped. "Luisa's just texted me their flight details. God, it's 7.15 am! I wish I hadn't offered to go and meet them now."

"Are you going to see if Jonas will take you?" asked Gudrun, predictably.

"No, it's better to keep work and...other things separate."

"Quite right. I try and stay well away from Olafur in similar situations."

"You know what I mean, you twit. Come on, let's get back to it."

"Do we need to sort anything for the new staff coming in tomorrow?"

"I think we told them to come in at 1 pm, didn't we? That'll give us chance to do the displays in the morning and then in the afternoon, perhaps we'll split them into two groups and one of us will show them the merchandising and one of us will train them on the till. But you should do the introduction and walk them around the store. After today I'm just your sidekick."

"It's about time I got to boss you around," laughed Gudrun, throwing a cushion at Rachel who chucked it straight back.

"Oi! I've been a great boss!"

"It has been great working together. I hope the new people are as much fun because otherwise, I'll really miss you."

"You'll miss me anyway."

"You're right. The constant ups and downs of your love life have been a highlight. I will miss hearing about all of that."

"Well, there might be nothing to hear once I go back to London," said Rachel glumly.

"No way! You and Jonas, neither of you are the types for a fling. I think you'll work out a way to be together in the end. Now, come on, we've got loads to do." Gudrun hauled herself off the sofa and ripped open the next box on the pile.

That evening, after they'd finished at the shop, Rachel went to the pool and Gudrun decided to tag along because Olafur was off on the tour with Jonas so she was at a bit of a loose end.

"I hardly ever do this," said Gudrun as they lay on their backs in the saltwater pool, staring at the sky. "It's so relaxing."

"Have you ever seen the Northern Lights?" asked Rachel as she tipped her head back to stare at the sky.

"Yes, of course. But I'm not sure I've ever seen them in

Reykjavik, not that I can remember anyway. Are you going to try and go on another Northern Lights tour before you leave?"

"I'd love to but I don't think I'll have the chance. I'm seeing Jonas tomorrow night and after that, I expect I'll be too busy working."

"That's such a shame but it's just another reason to come back again."

"There are so many reasons to come back again." But Jonas was right at the top of her list.

26

Seven-thirty the next morning felt far too early as Rachel wearily got dressed for the last day of titivating the store before the London contingent arrived the next day.

As she walked the short distance from the hotel to the shop, the streets were pretty much deserted and the shop was in darkness as the window lights hadn't been switched on yet. She opened the door and fumbled for the light switch, feeling an immense sense of satisfaction as she surveyed the stocked shelves; it looked almost ready to go.

Gudrun was not far behind her and had bought a very welcome coffee for them both. They strolled around talking about what needed doing that morning before the new staff arrived. The main things on their list were to dress the window sofa with cushions, dress the kitchen island and choose lampshades to display overhead. Gudrun had a lot of colour arranging that she wanted to do as well, but that was only if there was time.

"Right," said Rachel. "Why don't you pick out some cushions for the window sofa. You need to make sure they all go together, obviously, and try to avoid choosing all of your absolute favourites. Basically, anything that you put in the window will sell more so we need to choose some things which we think won't be naturally strong sellers."

Gudrun began picking out cushions while Rachel chose a selection of lampshades making sure she had different shapes and sizes but in colours that would complement each other.

By the time they stopped for lunch, they both felt that it looked good enough to be the opening day. It was ready. Gudrun went to Te & Kaffi to pick up some coffee and lunch while Rachel made sure the till was on and connected to the network ready for the training that afternoon.

There was a knock at the door and Rachel went across to open it wondering why Gudrun was knocking. Perhaps she couldn't manage to open the door while she was carrying lunch.

She flung the door open, "Sorry, I should have come with you...Adam!"

He was stood there. At the door of the shop. In Iceland.

"Hi Rachel," he said with a tight-lipped smile.

"What are you doing here?" she asked, standing aside to let him into the shop. She crossed her arms, feeling awkward, wondering whether they should hug or something. But no, better not to.

"I felt really bad about how everything happened and I just thought it would be better to talk face-to-face."

"But...I'm coming home in a few days. There was no need."

He was looking around the shop as she spoke.

"It looks like you've done a great job, Rach. It's just about ready then?"

"Yes, everyone's flying in tomorrow."

Gudrun came back with her hands full, opening the door with her bottom and walking in backwards.

"I got extra shots in our coffees ready for...oh, hello." She stopped talking and looked at Rachel, her eyebrows raised, waiting for an introduction.

"Oh, Gudrun, this is Adam. Adam, Gudrun, our store manager."

They shook hands and Rachel thought Gudrun was going to burst with curiosity. She could just imagine the grilling she was going to get when Adam left.

"Nice to meet you Gudrun."

"Yes, great to meet you, Adam. What brings you to Reykjavik?"

Rachel glared at Gudrun.

"Anyway, I must pop downstairs for some plates," she said, walking off, backwards again, mouthing silent 'Oh my Gods' to Rachel who tried not to look at her.

"Are you free for coffee later? Or dinner?" he asked. He looked good, smart as usual and despite everything, Rachel couldn't help feeling pleased to see him.

"It's bad timing. We're training new staff this afternoon and I'm going out tonight."

Rachel could feel herself blush as she tried to be vague over her date with Jonas later. Although she wasn't the one who had cheated, from Adam's point of view she could imagine it would look a bit suspect for her to be going out with someone else so soon.

"It's not something you could put off? I have come a long way to see you, Rach. It would be really good to talk."

Maybe she could meet Adam for a drink and then see Jonas later on.

"I'll text you when we finish here and we could meet for a drink."

"Great, I'll wait to hear from you then."

He turned and headed to the door. As he opened it, he looked around the store again and said, "It's really good to see you."

Almost the second the door closed, Gudrun came rushing up from the basement.

"*Guð minn góður*! What is he doing here?"

"He says he came to see me, to talk."

Rachel was stunned that now, after everything that had happened, now that it was over, he had actually surprised her and turned up, albeit unannounced and at almost the worst possible time. She was torn between giving him a chance to explain and sticking to her guns and wondered whether to call off dinner with Jonas so that she could allow Adam some proper time, given that he'd come all this way. But it was the last proper chance she would have to spend time with Jonas and was something that couldn't be put off until some other time, whereas Adam had just rocked up and now she was forced into having to hear him out when it could easily have waited until she was back in London.

"Aren't you seeing Jonas tonight?"

"Yes, but I'm going to meet Adam for a drink first. I mean he has come all this way to talk, I can't just not see him."

"No, I suppose not." Gudrun looked despondent. "But don't forget what he did, Rachel. And don't forget about Jonas."

"Gudrun, I'm not planning to forgive and forget with Adam just yet, but he deserves a chance to say his piece."

"Okay. I am just saying. I love you and Jonas together."

"I know," said Rachel hugging her. "Look, let's get ourselves ready for the newbies and try and focus on that for now."

"Oh, will I ever be as wise as you?" laughed Gudrun, as they made a start on their lunch before it was too late.

*

While Gudrun welcomed her team and got them organised, Rachel took a coffee order and popped along the road. When she got back Gudrun was doing a welcome speech in Icelandic, switching into English to introduce Rachel.

"Okay," Gudrun said, "let's walk the store."

Rachel smiled at her English retail expression which had left most of her staff looking bemused.

It was customary to 'walk the store' with a new shop to make sure everyone knew the space, the reasons for the merchandising decisions and to give them some idea of how the customer is likely to experience the store. They strolled around in a group with Gudrun, now solely speaking English, leading the way and Rachel only interjecting when Gudrun looked to her for clarification. Rachel was impressed with her manner; the three women and one young man were hanging onto her every word and seemed genuinely enthusiastic about the products. Once they had been shown around they split into two groups with Rachel taking the till training and Gudrun showing them the stock room and merchandising.

Every Monday, the marketing department sent each store the scheme for that week so, although they each had stock which was individual to them, there were broad guidelines about what should be included in the displays for every shop. There was usually a detailed plan for the main window and around 75% of the interior display space with 25% left to each store to use as promotion for their local products.

Rachel had printed off the scheme for the week and laid it all out on the counter. She explained to the team how to interpret the information and they allocated different areas to each person with Rachel and Gudrun taking the window together as that would normally be Gudrun's responsibility. Also, Rachel wasn't sure whether the Design Call would produce stock quickly enough for them to have at the opening so they decided to do all the displays with what they had rather than leaving any space unused as the London team would not like that at all. Besides, it was extra practice for everyone and gave them a chance to use their initiative rather than the whole thing being decided by Head Office.

They all got on with what they had to do. The atmosphere was light-hearted and there was a fair amount of banter, not always in English which was slightly worrying at times from Rachel's perspective – who knew what they were saying? The whole place had come together over the course of the day and Rachel felt so proud of it and keen to see what Luisa and everyone else thought when they arrived the next day.

All afternoon, Rachel was expecting Jonas to text her or call with firm arrangements for the evening. Eventually, she gave up waiting and texted him to say that she would meet him at her hotel at 8 pm. Hopefully, that would give her enough time to see Adam after work and still meet Jonas without having to rush.

"Hey, Gudrun, can I have a quick word?" Rachel called from the window, while the new staff were practising scanning stock on the till. "Have you heard from Olafur today?"

"He left me a voicemail to say they might be delayed because someone in the group has had an accident, nothing serious."

"I've been texting Jonas and he hasn't got back to me."

"They won't have any signal, Rachel. I expect Olafur rang on the satellite phone. They'll just have detoured to get the guest some medical help but they'll still be back today. You can try calling the satellite phone if you like? The number's in my phone."

"No, it's fine," said Rachel, feeling foolish. "I always forget about there being no signal."

27

By the time they left the shop, it was after 6 pm and Rachel had texted Adam and arranged to meet at Islenski Barinn. It had been easy to explain where it was and she could already see him sat in the window when she arrived. He stood up hurriedly as soon as he saw her. Rachel noticed straight away that he looked more attentive and less sure of himself than he usually did.

"Hi, I got you a glass of wine. I hope that's alright."

"It's great, thank you."

Rachel paused to look at him properly. Despite his slight nervousness, he looked just like normal. He was wearing wool trousers and a shirt and jumper underneath his tweedy jacket. Still smart. Still undeniably polished and although she hated herself for thinking it, still sexy.

"I can't believe you came."

"God, what a mess Rach," he said, shaking his head with his eyes not able to meet hers. "I am so sorry, really. It felt like the only way to make you see that was to come here, and not because I'm expecting you to forgive me, but because we've been together for too long to let it end without a proper conversation."

The way he said it was as if there had been no catalyst for the end of their relationship. Had he forgotten that *he* was the instigator of how it all inevitably ended?

"Adam, you surely didn't come here just to apologise."

He opened his mouth to reply but Rachel was too quick for him.

"You *kissed* someone else. And that's just what I know about."

"That's all there is to know. I was just so stressed out with work. I know that's no excuse, I do, but I wasn't myself after you left. I was under so much pressure, that's the reason I didn't manage to come the other weekend. It wasn't for any other reason, I promise. I lost all perspective and all I could think about was that I would lose my job if I wasn't at work to close that deal, and I would have Rach, believe me. But it made me realise that I didn't want to be dictated to by someone else. I've worked hard to get where I am and that has to mean something."

"So, you really have left Grainger Jones?"

"Yes. I told you," he said, looking confused.

"I know, it's just a big decision. I was surprised how quickly you made it, that's all."

"Jim had approached me about going into business together so it seemed like the ideal time and although it'll be hard work to get the new business off the ground we've got some great leads already and the best thing is that I won't be a slave to anyone else."

Rachel had to admit, he made it sound fantastic but in reality, she knew that Adam and Jim building a business together would mean even longer hours than before and the pressure of the work would be nothing compared to the pressure they'd both put on themselves to make a success of it.

"So, you think that changes things?" she said evenly.

"I think it's an explanation, yes."

"And nothing like this kissing business has ever happened before?"

"Not really, no."

"That's not a firm 'no', Adam."

"Well, you know. I'm trying to be honest, Rach and in that spirit, there may have been the odd drunken kiss but I swear that's all. And it was always work-related."

He thought that made it alright if it was in the name of schmoozing a client or closing a deal, but it completely revolted her.

"I appreciate your honesty," she said with a hint of sarcasm that made Adam instantly look ashamed, "but that is dreadful. I would not have dreamed of kissing anyone while we were together and I never thought you would be like that. It's as if you're a different person when you're not with me."

"It's because I'm not with you, Rach, and I want it to be

different. I want you by my side, building my business with me, doing it together, for us."

He reached across the table and touched her fingers with his. "Please, give me another chance. It was a mistake and I know I behaved badly but it can be different."

Rachel gazed out of the window. She didn't know what to think. Had she made the wrong decision after all because perhaps he did deserve another chance. It niggled her that despite being sure that she was keeping the idea of her and Jonas out of her decision about Adam, it had been a factor. How could it not have been? She turned to look at Adam but as she did, caught sight of someone in a red coat out of the corner of her eye.

"Can you excuse me for a sec?" she said, pulling her hand away from Adam's and going outside without putting her coat on.

"Jonas!" she called as he was walking away, with Olafur next to him who oddly enough was carrying both rucksacks. They must have just got back from the trip. When Jonas turned around, Rachel saw that his left arm was in a sling and he looked extremely pale, even from a distance. She ran towards him, stopping short of an embrace in case she hurt him.

"What happened to you? Gudrun said someone had an accident but we thought it was a guest."

"One of my crampons came loose when we were hiking and I slipped and fell on my shoulder. I have broken my *viðbein*; I don't know the English word," he said, gesturing to his shoulder.

"Collarbone?"

"Yes, collarbone. It will be fine in a few weeks."

"Are you feeling alright though? Is it painful?"

"It is not too bad now but when it happened..." he closed his eyes and shuddered slightly. "It is okay now, I'm okay."

Olafur rolled his eyes, clearly thinking that Jonas wasn't alright at all, but he said nothing and moved away to look into a shop window.

Jonas looked tenderly into Rachel's eyes, making her stomach flutter. Then, noticing she was shivering said, "Rachel it's freezing, where is your coat?"

He took Rachel's hand in his and held it to his chest rubbing his thumb against the back of her hand.

"I was just having a drink in Islenksi Barinn when I saw you walk past."

"It's great to see you, sorry I didn't call you. I was waiting until I got back," he said with a weak smile. He bent forward to kiss her.

"Hi, I don't think we've met, I'm Adam."

Adam was stood behind Rachel, holding his hand out to Jonas to shake. Rachel instinctively moved away from Jonas, staring in disbelief at Adam.

"Jonas."

They shook hands. Jonas looked surprised and briefly raised his eyebrow to Rachel as if to ask what was going on.

"Rachel spotted you while we were having a drink. You look like you've been in the wars."

"It's not as bad as it looks."

"She's told me a lot about you. You're the tour guide?"

She had hardly told him anything about Jonas. Adam was trying to stake his claim over her and even though she could see what was happening, she couldn't think of anything to say. It was as if she was watching it from afar, powerless to intervene.

"Yes, that's right."

"It's his company," said Rachel.

That was all she could manage to say in defence of Jonas who seemed to be visibly waning as they stood there.

"Of course. It was great to meet you but we'd better be getting back inside before we freeze. Rachel?"

Adam took a couple of steps back towards the bar and was waiting for her to follow him

"I'll call you later," said Jonas.

"Actually Jonas, we're in the middle of something. Rachel didn't know I was coming to visit and we have a lot to catch up on."

Jonas looked at Rachel to see if she was going to speak up for herself but she just looked at him with an agonised expression.

"Hey Jonas," Olafur said, having re-joined his friend. "Let's go."

They walked away slowly with Olafur putting his arm under Jonas's good arm to support him.

Rachel followed Adam back into the warmth of Islenski Barinn. She was mortified that Adam and Jonas had met like that, but now that she was over the shock, she was furious that she had allowed Adam to take charge of the situation. They sat down at the table again, Adam reaching for her hand across the table as if nothing had interrupted them.

"How dare you speak to him like that?" she said angrily, trying to keep her voice down.

"I didn't come all this way to watch you go off into the sunset with some other bloke. I assume you're seeing him? Jonas?"

"We're friends."

"With benefits?"

"Oh God, Adam! Really? That is hardly the way to win me back. I mean five minutes ago you were all sweetness and light, 'I'm so sorry Rachel, it was a mistake, Rachel' and now... well, maybe this is the side of you I've never really known."

"Don't be melodramatic," he said drily. "I just thought two years of our lives together were worth more than a Skype break-up."

Rachel felt a blush of shame creep up her body. He was right, perhaps she hadn't been fair. He deserved a chance to put things right and however much Rachel told herself that she *had* been perfectly fair, now that he was here, in front of her, it was harder for her to feel at ease with that.

"Okay. Give me a couple of minutes."

She went to the ladies and rang Jonas. He deserved an explanation, but his phone went to voicemail.

"Hi, it's Rachel. I am so sorry about what happened earlier. I didn't know Adam was coming and now, well I feel like I have to let him have his chance to explain as he came all this way. Please call me, I need to see you. I'm so sorry, I hope you're okay."

Rachel returned to the table ready to let Adam say his piece, but first, she was going to say hers. She was sure that nothing he could say would change her mind but let him try if he wanted to. He was so arrogant towards Jonas and after what he'd done, what Anna had seen, he had no business being possessive or jealous.

"Look, I know that breaking up on Skype wasn't great but I was hoping to talk things through on the weekend when you were supposed to visit, so I felt like I had no choice. That wasn't how I wanted things to end but I needed some closure and I didn't think I could wait until I got back to London. It never crossed my mind that you would cheat on me, Adam and I won't be with someone who treats me like that."

Now that her shock at Adam and Jonas meeting had subsided, she felt empowered and able to calmly reason with Adam.

"I'm pleased for you that you've started your own business if that's what you want but if we were partners you would have spoken to me about that. It's a decision which would affect us both far more than me coming to Iceland and you had plenty to say about that."

"You're right, Rach, about everything. What about a fresh start when you come back home? We can start again. It'll be like it was in the early days, let's fall in love with each other again."

He looked sincere, his eyes were sparkling behind his glasses and Rachel saw a glimpse of the old Adam who she had fallen for in the beginning. But this time, she felt different and she knew deep down that it would be a mistake to try and start recreating something which hadn't been so perfect the first time. She realised that she had no feelings for him anymore. There was affection but where there had been love there was just a faint memory of something that had felt like love at the time but which she now knew wasn't.

"No. It's over. You have to accept that. Do you want to be with a person who doesn't trust you anymore?"

"I think we can get past that."

"I can't and I don't want to."

That was the truth. She didn't want to try. For her, there was nothing worth trying to hold onto.

"Look, I'm staying at the Hotel Borg. Let's have lunch tomorrow."

"I'm not having lunch with you, Adam. You should go back to London."

She stood up and pulled her coat on as he looked her in disbelief.

"Rachel."

"Bye Adam. I'll call you when I get back."

She walked to the corner of the street then stopped and wondered what to do next. She desperately wanted to see Jonas but wasn't sure she could remember the way to his house. She pulled her phone out and called him but his phone was off.

It was somewhere in the very middle of town, she knew that. Maybe she would find it if she wandered up and down a few streets.

Was it mad to think that what she felt for Jonas was love – already? It was the only way she could explain how the love she thought she and Adam had shared wasn't the real thing because she had a strong inkling that what she and Jonas could have if they let it happen, was love.

Turning a corner and finding a garden full of twinkling lights and trolls, Rachel recognised Jonas's house. It was in darkness but she knocked on the door just in case. No answer. She sat down on the doorstep and scrolled through her phone to find Gudrun's number. There was a good chance that Jonas was at their house, but again, there was no answer.

By the time Rachel fell into bed later that night, she was exhausted and emotionally drained. She hadn't heard from Jonas and she didn't blame him. She should never have let Adam monopolise the situation to the point where she had abandoned Jonas in favour of hearing Adam out. What must Jonas think? She could have ruined everything.

28

For the first time since she had arrived in Iceland, Rachel dressed up for work like she normally would. There was no more hauling of boxes or climbing up ladders to be done now so she could afford to wear a dress and not snow boots for a change. She knew that although there was still lying snow everywhere, the pavements were clear so she decided to risk wearing her black patent brogues.

For once, she ate breakfast downstairs in the hotel which was very relaxing and quiet at 6 am. She had cup after cup of tea and scanned through her emails. The London flight was due to arrive on time and Rachel had arranged to go and meet them at the airport with a minibus, as there would be five of them plus the luggage.

Stood by herself in the arrivals hall, Rachel realised how nervous she was. Julia and Dave always unnerved her a little bit because being the founders, everyone was slightly in awe of them. Well, apart from Luisa who had no problem telling someone if she disagreed with them, whoever they were. It occurred to Rachel that she ought to have bought a sign to hold up as she was somewhat disguised in her big coat and knitted hat. She pulled her hat off just in case.

A slow trickle of people started to come through and Rachel saw them before they saw her. Luisa was togged up to the nines in fleeces, snow boots and she had a deerstalker hat in her hand. Stella, the Snug marketing and branding manager, had given a nod to the fact that it might be cold by wearing some Uggs but the others were dressed for a normal day at the office. Rachel regretted not having given them a heads-up about what to bring; it hadn't even crossed her mind and it was too late now.

"Rachel!"

No need for a card after all, Luisa had spotted her straight away. Rachel headed over to them, gave Luisa a hug and air-kissed Julia, Dave and Stella. They all looked excited, probably the same way she had been when she'd arrived. The driver who must have been lurking behind her appeared from nowhere and started helping with the luggage.

"Welcome to Iceland! We've got the minibus just outside, it's not far but you'll probably want to put your coats on," Rachel advised.

"Christ, it's bloody freezing." An astute observation by Dave.

Rachel would never admit to anyone that she thought he was a bit of a hanger-on. Julia was the founder and he'd just gone along with it and was not at all business-minded and sometimes not all that bright in general. Rachel was pretty sure that's what everyone else thought too but it was safer not to mention it.

"Oh my God, the snow will ruin my boots," said Stella, dispelling the myth that Uggs were practical winter footwear.

"Don't worry, the paths are all clear in town and the minibus is just over there so we can avoid the snow. It's more like compact ice now anyway." Rachel was pleased with herself for sounding like a local.

On the way to Reykjavik, she sat in the back of the minibus with everyone else, pointing out all the things she could remember Jonas telling her on her first trip along the same road. It was, at the moment, a bright sunny day so Iceland was looking at its best.

Everyone was staying in the same hotel as Rachel so she helped to get them booked in at reception while Dave and the driver bought all the luggage in. They agreed to meet back in the lobby in half an hour. Rachel decided to dash along to Te & Kaffi and grab a coffee. It would have been better if it was a stiff gin and tonic to help calm her butterflies, but it was still a bit early for that and besides, she needed all her wits about her. There were bound to be tons of questions and decisions that she'd have to explain – that she'd already explained to Luisa so it would be just for show, for the benefit of Julia.

As they walked into the store together an hour later, Rachel watched for their reaction and it was perfect. Julia grinned and that was the cue for everyone else to start saying it all looked great. They walked the store beginning with the left-hand side where there were vases, lampshades and candles all stacked on the Snug trademark black wire shelving with rough wood panelling on the walls as a neutral background to everything. Rachel was most proud of the lampshade display area where they had different coloured electrical cables coming down from the ceiling ending at varying heights, lower near the wall and higher above the thoroughfare, allowing them to switch the shades regularly to show off the stock and change the look to keep things fresh. It hadn't been done in any of their stores before, it had been Rachel's idea and if she said so herself, it looked great. And everyone else thought so too. The back of the store was the kitchen area where they had the island unit and lots of crockery, mugs, chopping boards, placemats and things like that. Along the right -hand side of the store was the slightly relocated counter unit which she did have to justify to Julia, and then the living room zone with Gudrun's rainbow display of cushions.

Gudrun had walked around with them, answering some of their questions along with Rachel. Before they'd arrived, she'd lit some candles and brewed some coffee so the shop had just the right ambience and smelt wonderful. The windows still had the coverings on so it was hard to imagine what it would look like the next day with natural light flooding in but for now, it was cosy and welcoming, just how you'd want your home to be.

Dave announced that he was going exploring and wanted Julia to go with him. She was reluctant because she wanted to stay and go over the arrangements for the Design Call that was due to start later in the morning but Stella persuaded her that she and Rachel would go through and plan everything and brief her later. As soon as they'd left, everyone breathed a sigh of relief that they didn't have to be on their best behaviour anymore.

Stella, Luisa and Rachel flopped onto the sofa, the last day that they'd be able to do that without becoming a window display themselves, and started to plan for the logistics of the Design Call. Rachel and Gudrun couldn't help much as regards how many people they would be expecting but Stella had already picked up a bit of a buzz about it on social media so she thought there would be a fair number of people. Gudrun, Julia and Stella would see each person for five minutes or so in the office and the rest of the staff would keep the queue - hopefully, there would be a queue - happy on the shop floor.

All morning, Gudrun had been noticeably cool towards Rachel, a sign that she had heard about what had happened last night. Rachel pulled her aside at the first opportunity.

"Is Jonas staying with you and Olafur?"

"Yes. He needs looking after."

"Did he tell you what happened last night?"

Gudrun nodded.

"Is he alright?"

Gudrun mellowed when she realised the level of Rachel's concern.

"He is very down. He is in a lot of pain and he's upset about not being able to work. And he's upset about last night."

"It was awful, Gudrun, and I feel so desperately bad about the whole thing. I just let Adam warn him off and I didn't say anything. I was so shocked that they were stood there together, it was like it slowed my brain down and it was all over before I realised. What did he say?"

"He didn't say much, Olafur told me what happened. Jonas was exhausted and he looked dreadful, Rachel."

Rachel's heart lurched at the thought of him injured and on top of that, thinking she had rejected him.

"He won't answer my calls. Can I go round and see him at your house?"

"Yes, of course. But be gentle with him, Rachel."

She would be. All she wanted was to hold him, let him know that it was him she wanted, that Adam had been throwing his weight around but that it really was over between them. She needed to make sure he knew that and then they could grab every spare second that was left before she went home.

Julia and Dave reappeared an hour later raving about how amazing the town was, by which time Gudrun and Stella had got the office ready for the Design Call.

"Rachel, can we grab five minutes with Luisa and Dave," said Julia, speaking to the whole shop as she said it. The four of them trooped downstairs to the office. Julia perched on the desk, Dave stood at her shoulder with Rachel and Luisa waiting in silence while she checked her phone.

"Sorry about that," she said as she pushed her phone into her back pocket. "Okay, I have some exciting news."

She looked at Dave who gave her a nod of encouragement.

"We've been approached by a buyer. Someone interested in buying the company."

Rachel and Luisa looked at each other in shock which told them straight away that it was news to both of them. Suddenly, the mention of the business consultant in Julia's phone call began to make sense.

"It's a huge high street retailer who wants to get into the handmade market. They're impressed with our growth in the UK and our plans for expansion overseas."

At that moment, Gudrun knocked and came into the room with Adam behind her.

"Adam, I can't talk now, I'm in a meeting," said Rachel calmly, trying to convey to him with her eyes how inappropriate it was for him to have come to the shop, today of all days.

"Oh, you two know each other?" said Julia. "Well, that makes things easier. Luisa, this is Adam Kempton from Finch Associates."

"Great to meet you, Luisa. Dave, Julia…Rachel." He went through each name in turn as he shook hands with everyone.

"So, Adam is going to spend the next couple of days with us on behalf of the buyer. They're keen to see how we work, how we launch our stores and crucially, how we source our stock. I should tell you that pending a successful outcome, fingers crossed," Julia said crossing her fingers and grinning at Adam, "we will be going ahead with the sale imminently."

"How will that affect everyone?" asked Luisa.

"In the short term, the buyer plans to keep all existing staff pending a review," began Adam. "In my experience, they will keep most of the key staff so as not to disrupt the success model of the business."

Rachel stared at him. It was as if last night had never happened. Now he was in work mode. And then it hit her. He had come here *for work.* He hadn't come to see her at all. He was coming *anyway.*

"Rachel, perhaps you could walk the store with Adam, seeing as you two know each other," beamed Julia, clearly oblivious to the fact that Rachel was glaring at Adam with a look that could kill. "We'll get ready for the Design Call."

"Who knows about the sale? What about Stella and Gudrun?" asked Luisa, barely disguising her contempt as she addressed Julia.

"I'd prefer it if we can keep it within this store for now. By the time we get back to London, it will be confirmed. You can tell Stella and Gudrun if necessary."

Rachel led the way upstairs, still reeling from Julia's announcement about the sale of Snug but more from the fact that *that* was why Adam was here. It was always going to be about work and he hadn't mentioned anything about working on Snug last night. Even if it was a secret he could have told her he was visiting for work instead of insisting that he had come purely to see her. Looking back, it had seemed so out of character and now Rachel knew exactly what she was dealing with.

"I can't believe I thought you had come to see me," she said, marching Adam to the back of the store, away from the gathering queue of designers being organised by Gudrun's staff over by the entrance.

"It was a coincidence. Obviously, we needed to talk so when it came up that Jim or I needed to come over for the opening, I offered. It doesn't mean I wouldn't have come anyway."

"Of course it does! I'm such a bloody idiot. I should have known there was no way you would come here just to make up with me. Do you know, I've learned more about you in four weeks of being apart than I ever did in two years together."

"Hang on a minute," he interjected, "you've lost all sense of perspective since you've been here. Nothing changed between us except that you left and-"

"And I can see what life can be like, Adam, if work isn't the number one priority. That's what's changed. I've changed and that's why it's not going to work with us anymore."

"Look, Rach, I'm here to do a job and it needs doing and so does yours. So let's put this aside and just get on with it."

That said it all. She would get through this day and she would go and see Jonas and apologise to him.

29

Somehow, Rachel managed to walk the store with Adam by pretending that he was someone she didn't know. Not much pretending required, as she felt as if she didn't know him now. She cut herself off from all the emotions that were swimming inside her and focused. She was professional, answered his questions even though she couldn't help thinking that if he'd ever been listening when she'd talked to him about her day, he'd already know a lot of the answers.

When he finally set up his laptop on the kitchen island to make some notes, Rachel took a deep breath and went to see how the queue was doing. It didn't bother her that she wasn't involved in the pitches because she much preferred meeting the designers while they were waiting, more relaxed, not thinking they had to impress anyone, and she loved hearing their stories which they might not have time to tell in their five-minute spot.

The first girl in the queue was wearing a fantastic heavy knitted jacket with a knitted headband, presumably instead of a hat. She had long blonde hair and had a large holdall with her.

"Hi, I'm Rachel, I work for Snug in London."

She stood up to shake hands.

"You're number one in the queue," Rachel said, stating the obvious, "what have you brought with you?"

"I'm Eldey, I have bought woven blankets from Icelandic Lopi wool."

Rachel immediately remembered Katrin from the wool shop

mentioning someone who wove blankets; it must be her. She unzipped the holdall and pulled out a blanket which was in the most beautiful colours Rachel had ever seen. It was soft heathery shades mixed with a smoky black which sounded strange but it was wonderful.

"Gosh, that's stunning."

It was not that soft when Rachel came to touch it but she had already discovered that Icelandic yarn is quite rugged and made for warmth rather than tactility. Over time it softens down as you wear or use it.

"Thank you. It is the colours from the lava fields in the summer when the wildflowers bloom."

This was just what they were after; something local which had a great story. Something that people could link to Iceland when they'd gone home or if they lived here, a beautiful reminder of the summer in the dark winter months. Rachel felt pretty sure that number one in the queue would be a 'yes' which would be the best possible start to the Design Call.

The brand-new coffee machine was in overdrive and Rachel had already spotted several more items that she hoped they would say yes to. But now, she was free to sneak out to visit Jonas. She went to find her coat and found Luisa sat in the stock room typing into her phone.

"Rachel, tell me you did not know about this sale business."

"I didn't. I spoke to Julia the other day and she said a business consultant was coming with you but I didn't know why and I didn't know it was Adam."

"Really, he didn't mention it?"

"No, he honestly didn't. We've broken up so we've not been talking but I saw him yesterday and he said he'd come here to see me. It was just as much of a shock to me as it was for you."

"It was completely out of the blue, wasn't it? I'm amazed Julia's managed to keep it quiet. There's been no hint of anything going on at all back in the office. And whatever he says, I can't help but worry about how secure our jobs are."

Rachel wanted to be able to reassure Luisa but she had heard Adam talk about enough takeovers to know that often the top people in the company were the first ones to be replaced by the buyer's people.

"I suppose we just have to get on with it and see what happens," said Rachel.

"I'm putting out a few feelers," Luisa said, waving her phone. "If Julia can spring that on us without so much as a hint, my loyalty to Snug can be equally fickle."

"I'm just popping out for a bit," said Rachel, shrugging her coat on. "I think they're fine to get on without me for a bit."

"Okay, see you later. Hopefully, I'll have a job offer by the time you get back," she said rolling her eyes.

"It might not come to that, you know. If they want to continue with the roll-out of new stores, you're key to that. There's no way they can bring in an outsider who would be able to do that job."

Rachel left, armed with directions to Gudrun's house. It wasn't far away, just a five-minute walk. She was so nervous about seeing Jonas after what had happened and tried to tell herself that it would be alright. Jonas was nothing if not easy-going and hopefully, he would be willing to hear her out.

Gudrun's house was the epitome of a cosy but traditional Icelandic cottage. It was one-storey clad in blue with white windows and a grey roof. The fence outside was laced with fairy lights, just like Jonas's, and the glow from the small windows made it look very inviting.

Rachel went up the steps and knocked on the door. Her heart was beating so hard that she felt like she might pass out so she took a couple of deep breaths to try and calm herself down.

The door opened and Jonas stood there. His hair was more tousled than usual and he was still pale with dark circles under his eyes. His left arm in its sling was hidden underneath his knitted Icelandic Lopi sweater.

"Come in," he said wearily, closing the door behind her. Rachel took off her boots and left them by the door.

The small hallway opened into the lounge which was furnished with two sofas either side of a wood-burning stove, there were bright rugs and cushions everywhere. The walls were filled with photographs in mismatched frames of all colours and sizes and various lamps cast an intimate light across the room.

Jonas lowered himself into the corner of one sofa, wincing as he did so and catching his breath.

"How are you feeling?"

"Not too good."

The sparkle had gone from his eyes and Rachel was alarmed to see how broken he looked. It was a million miles away from the Jonas she knew.

"Can I get you anything?"

"A glass of water and some painkillers would be great. They're in the kitchen."

Rachel went through the only other door in the room into a larger hallway which opened out into a kitchen where she found various boxes of medication on the table. She got a glass of water and took a few packets of the pills back into the lounge.

"I didn't know which ones," she said, holding them in front of him. He took one of the packets from her and proceeded to try and extricate the tablets with one hand.

"I can do that," said Rachel gently, taking them from him.

He swallowed the pills and sat with his eyes closed for a couple of minutes.

"Sorry," he said finally. "I hate being stuck inside not able to do anything."

"I bet," said Rachel, thinking that it must be like torture for Jonas who was outdoors virtually all of the time. "And please, don't apologise. I came to apologise to you. I am so sorry, Jonas, about yesterday. Adam just turned up out of the blue so I went for a drink with him just to hear him out and then…well, you know. I shouldn't have let him speak to you like that, it was just such a shock when he came outside and saw us."

"It's not your fault, Rachel. It is natural for him to want to fight for you and that is what he was doing." He looked resigned to it.

"But that's not why he came at all. We found out at the shop this morning that Snug is being bought out and Adam came here on behalf of the buyer. For work, not for me. And it really is over, Jonas. Whatever he says, it's over. And I'm sorry I didn't say that last night in front of both of you. I'm sorry I abandoned you last night when we were supposed to be together."

"I was going to have to cancel dinner anyway," he said nodding at his shoulder. "I wouldn't have been very good company last night." He attempted a smile but his mouth barely moved and his eyes showed he didn't mean it.

"Look, I know I'm leaving in a couple of days and it feels like time is running out for us, but I want you to know that nothing has changed for me. I like you, Jonas. I know you're hurt and feeling bad, but could I just come and be with you tonight? We've got a work thing but…"

"Rachel," he said softly. "I think it's too late. We had a great time, but we both agreed that it would only go on while you were here and we've run out of time. I would have loved to show you the Northern Lights before you left but now I can't. I can't do anything now so we should say goodbye."

His eyes were watering and it was all that Rachel could do to stop herself from sobbing and throwing herself into his arms.

"Jonas, it isn't too late. We have something special and we could make it work. London isn't that far."

"I can't do a long-distance relationship again, it's too hard. It is not fair for either of us, it would be just like me and Sylvie all over again. We have to accept that we had a great time together and that now it is over." The tears were beginning to roll down his cheeks as he spoke but he kept his voice steady. "It would always have had to be like that, we knew. All we have missed is a couple of nights together and that would just make it harder to say goodbye. This is probably better for us both."

"It doesn't feel better, it feels shit," sobbed Rachel. "If only Adam hadn't come, it would have been alright. You wouldn't be doing this then."

"It's the right thing to do. Last night just made me realise that it's not meant to be with us. In the long run, this will save us both from worse hurt."

Rachel felt like there was nothing she could say to that. The last thing she wanted was for Jonas to be hurt any more than he already was and if spending more time together now was going to make anything worse for him, she wasn't going to risk it even if it hurt her infinitely more.

She went over and gently sat down next to him, taking his hand in hers.

"You're so special, Jonas. If it wasn't that we have only met each other four weeks ago, I would be telling you that I love you."

They both smiled through their tears and Rachel stroked the tears off Jonas's cheek and kissed him tenderly.

"I've had the time of my life here, thank you."

Then without looking back, she left.

Needing time to compose herself, Rachel headed to the sea. She wanted to take great lungfuls of sea air because she felt like she couldn't breathe properly. She didn't think Jonas was right; she couldn't hurt worse than she did now even if they'd spent more time together, fallen more deeply for each other. But she could see he was trying to save himself and she couldn't argue with that. She had seen for herself that he was in the depths of despair because of her, because of his accident and there was no turning that around in a couple of days. She had to go along with what he wanted.

When Rachel was little and they went to the seaside on holiday, as soon as they got out of the car her dad would make them inhale as hard as they could to breathe in the sea air. They must have looked like complete loons but it was a family tradition which, in a flash of nostalgia, Rachel remembered as she repeated the ritual now, gazing across the lagoon to the snow-capped mountains.

"What are you doing?"

"Oh my God, you made me jump!" She smacked her hand onto her chest as she turned around to see Olafur looking concerned. "I'm just breathing in the sea air," she explained feeling like a complete idiot.

"So am I," he grinned, "but look, I can do it with my normal breathing."

"Very funny."

"So, you have been to see Jonas?"

"Yes, he's not doing too good, is he?"

"He is frustrated. It is difficult to be injured for an active person. I expect you cheered him up."

"I don't know about that." Rachel rummaged for a tissue to blow her nose. "We've said goodbye. It was hard."

"He found it hard when Hilde left, he thinks that is what is happening this time. But it is different with you. He wasn't scared to take the risk until yesterday. I think he is not thinking clearly. That is what Gudrun says."

Rachel smiled at the thought of Olafur and Gudrun debating her and Jonas's relationship.

"The thing is, I can't expect him to feel any different. I understand how hard it is and he has no fight in him. I'm leaving in two days and he doesn't want to see me again, it has to be his choice."

"He is in pain, Rachel. He is not thinking clearly but he loves you."

The tears started running down Rachel's cheeks again. Olafur gathered her into a big hug.

"It will be alright in the end," he said.

"It already is the end."

30

By the time Rachel got back to the shop, there were still a few people waiting for the Design Call but the end was in sight. Luisa was perched on a stool, working away with her laptop on the kitchen island display unit. Thankfully Adam was nowhere to be seen,

"How has it gone?" Rachel asked her, taking off her coat.

"Really well from what I can gather. I had a word with Julia and she's very impressed."

"Oh, brilliant. The first thing I saw this morning I'd have said yes to."

Luisa's eyes lit up. "The woven blankets! I know! They must have said yes to her otherwise I'll have to hunt that woman down myself so I can buy one."

"I think she knows the lady who runs the wool shop so she would be easy to find. Where's Adam gone?"

"I think he's gone back to his hotel. He's going out with Julia and Dave tonight."

Rachel was relieved. After what had happened at Gudrun's, the last person she wanted to see was Adam. He'd probably be at the opening but hopefully, it would be too busy for them to be able to talk.

"Have Gudrun and Stella wondered why he's here yet?"

"They haven't had the chance. They've been holed up with Julia since you left." She looked at Rachel and frowned. "Have you been crying? Is everything alright, Rachel?"

"I'm fine. It's just been quite stressful with me and Adam, you know."

"Well, I can guess. It's quite something to find out your employer is selling up let alone to find out your boyfriend, sorry, ex-boyfriend, knew all about it and didn't tell you."

If Luisa thought that was a believable explanation, Rachel was happy to go along with it.

The Design Call was over. Gudrun had taken photos of all the samples they had been shown and had filed them into yes's and no's. Luckily for Luisa, the blankets were in the yes file. They all looked through the photos, oohing and ahhing over the beautiful things that Snug Reykjavik was going to be stocking. Some of the designers had stock available for the opening which meant shuffling around the existing stock to accommodate it but it was all part of the fun and meant that there would be no time for anyone to be nervous tomorrow.

Dave and Julia had booked somewhere expensive to eat that night, possibly because Adam would pick up the bill, thought Rachel cynically, so she, Luisa, Stella and Gudrun planned to eat out together. Rachel and Gudrun had decided that they would start by going to a fantastic fish and chip restaurant and then they'd go to the gin bar down by the harbour. They had closed up the shop as soon as the Design Call had finished so Rachel decided to go for a swim before they met for dinner. She needed to clear her head. Luisa was heading back to the hotel for a long bubble bath but Stella asked if she could tag along with Rachel.

Stella and Rachel had never really done anything together outside of work before, mainly because marketing didn't tend to get involved on-site for store launches until the opening and even then they were not often there at the same time so they didn't know each other that well. Plus, Stella had only been at Snug for a year and a half so there hadn't been many chances to socialise together.

Having a swimming buddy was a welcome distraction for Rachel and she was looking forward to seeing what Stella thought of the whole Icelandic swimming ritual. She was pretty fashionable and well put-together which made Rachel think she'd probably baulk at the idea of showering naked even more than she had. As it was, she was a little wide-eyed when Rachel told her but she took it in her stride as they purposely averted their eyes from each other until they'd got their cossies on. Rachel took her into the sitting pool first so they'd be warm while she pointed out the various options then Rachel went into the big pool to swim a few lengths. When she padded quickly across to the saltwater pool Stella was already relaxing in there so Rachel waded across to sit next to her.

"This is amazing, Rachel. How did you find out about it?" she asked lazily.

"The guy that picked me up from the airport told me. I was coming most evenings while we were doing the building work. It's so relaxing and I love swimming outside."

"I keep thinking I am glimpsing a flash of the Northern Lights," Stella said staring at the sky.

"I know. I always look for them but apparently, it's unusual to see them in the city because of the light pollution."

"Hmm. It's a shame we won't have time to go on a trip or something."

"I went on a Northern Lights trip when I first got here but the weather turned and we got caught in a snowstorm so I never did see them."

She thought back in fondness at that night with Jonas. A disaster that turned out to be anything but.

"Really? What happened? Did you all make it back to the city?"

"Well, it was just me and the tour guide because it was a private tour, I mean Adam was meant to be with us but... had missed his flight." Stella didn't need to know all the facts. "Luckily the guide knew somewhere we could stay and ride out the storm."

"Adam that was there today? I didn't know he was your boyfriend."

"Well, he's not now."

"Because he stood you up and left you to get stranded in a snowstorm?" said Stella playfully. "Sorry. That isn't why, is it?"

"No, not really. There were lots of reasons."

"So, what happened in the storm? God, what was the tour guide like? What a nightmare to be stranded with a virtual stranger."

Rachel smiled at Stella's stream-of-consciousness way of talking.

"It was okay. We just hunkered down in the cabin, lit a fire and waited until we could leave the next day."

"Ooh, Rachel, that's romantic! Was he nice, the tour guide?"

"Yes, he's lovely. We're friends now, actually."

"I should think you are," she said with a glint in her eye.

"Not like that," Rachel smiled, although it *had* been like that in the end… no-one needed to know about her and Jonas.

"Rachel! God, I could do with a bit of luck like that. My love life is a dearth of eligible men, you've got a lovely man at home and then that happens as well."

"I was cheesed off with Adam for not coming over, so I was happy to spend a cosy night with someone who didn't mind being with me. But he was too much of a gentleman to take advantage of that."

"I suppose a holiday fling isn't the best thing to do just because you're pissed off," Stella said. "You're probably relieved now that nothing happened."

"Mmm," Rachel said closing her eyes and sinking further into the water.

Later that evening after they had eaten at the fish and chip place, which was a huge hit with everyone, they strolled along to the harbour. Stella and Luisa both thought the same as Rachel had when Jonas took her there: there's nothing there. Then they turned the corner and saw the lit doorway and Stella practically broke into a run shouting, "Oh my God, Rachel, it looks so cool!" and "Wow! I didn't think there'd be anywhere like this!" when they hadn't even set foot in the place yet. Luckily, Rachel knew that the inside was not going to let them down.

They found a booth underneath the mezzanine and Rachel left them there while she and Gudrun went to the bar. They had decided on gin cocktails to begin with which seemed to be very labour intensive to make so she began gazing around while she was waiting, half expecting, hoping, to see Jonas, even though she knew it was wishful thinking.

"Did you really get stuck in a snowstorm with some hunk of an Icelandic tour guide?" asked Luisa when Rachel got back to the table, leaving Gudrun to wait for the rest of the drinks.

She shouldn't have left them alone. Clearly, Stella was not a natural confidant having taken less than five minutes to tell Luisa. Rachel knew they should have had straight gin and tonics, then she would have been quicker at the bar.

"Well, sort of. And he's not some hunk. Where did you get that from?" Rachel said, glaring at Stella. "God, it's like Chinese whispers."

"Alright, so you didn't *say* hunk but most of the guys I've seen here match that description," she grinned.

"That's just because they seem new and exciting compared to London men," said Luisa with her typical cynicism, "underneath they're all the same."

"Not *all* the same," Stella giggled.

It was a long time since Rachel had had a girls' night out, especially one with conversations like this, and it took her a little while to relax into the easy banter.

"Let's stick to the matter in hand," insisted Luisa, "spill the beans, Rachel. I could do with some vicarious romance."

Rachel re-told the story just as she'd already told Stella, only adding benign details like the place she'd had dinner that night and that Jonas had slept on the sofa. Yes, they'd both slept on the sofa but it was better to tame down that side of things because you never knew who they'd tell. Stella could be best friends with someone Adam knew or something, which wouldn't help anything.

"So that's why you and Adam split up?" Luisa asked Rachel.

"No, it was just the straw that broke the camel's back I suppose. Things hadn't been right for a while and it was easier to see that from here somehow."

"So, I don't get it. What was Adam doing here today? What's his job?" asked Stella. Luisa and Rachel looked at each other.

"He doesn't work for Snug does he?" asked Gudrun.

"No, he doesn't. And this has to stay between us. It cannot go any further." Rachel aimed that at Stella. "Snug is probably being sold. Adam's here working on behalf of the buyer."

"Oh my God! Are we all getting made redundant?" said Stella, gasping and holding her hand to her chest melodramatically.

"Well, we don't know, but he said not. He said they'd probably keep people on," said Rachel as Luisa rolled her eyes and took a swig of her cocktail.

"Oh, dear. So, it could be over before it's started," said Gudrun.

"I don't think they'll mess around with the staff in the stores because they'll want things to keep going as they are, at least for now. We need to remember that they're buying the successful company which we have built and there's no point in them buying it and then tearing it apart." Rachel tried to sound reassuring but she didn't know any better than anyone else. "Come on guys, let's try and enjoy ourselves. It's the big day tomorrow! We've worked hard on this store, we deserve a good night out. Skál!"

"Skál!" said Gudrun, joining in straight away. "Skál!" she said again gesturing for the others to join in. Eventually, everyone had clinked everyone else and they vowed not to talk about work anymore.

"Hey, Gudrun," began Stella, "is your boyfriend Icelandic?"

"He's a hunky Icelandic tour guide, Stella!" said Rachel, finally feeling able to let herself go. Gudrun laughed and nodded to confirm that was true.

"Oh my God, I need to go on one of these tours," groaned Stella.

31

The Grand Opening day had arrived at last. Rachel was wearing her black dress, woolly tights and brogues and she felt all sparkly and excited. She loved opening day. It was usually so busy that she got to work in the shop like a proper member of staff and it was the only time that she ever really came into contact with Snug customers. It was fantastic fun chatting to people and helping them choose things.

Gudrun had the whole thing planned like a military operation and had called her entire team in for the day. She had two of them on the tills, one stationed on the door to welcome customers and hand out baskets, two people tasked with keeping the shelves stocked and tidy and the rest of the team, including Julia, Luisa and Stella mingling and helping on the shop floor. Dave had gone by himself on a whale watching trip from the harbour because Julia, in her words, only had to look at a boat to be seasick.

Rachel picked at the corner of the window vinyl trying not to be annoyed with Gudrun who was picking away at the vinyl on the next pane. It was such an immensely satisfying job that Rachel wanted to do all of it herself. They peeled it off and finally glimpsed the outside world from inside the shop. Rachel went outside and stood across the road taking in the shopfront in all its glory and even to her it looked tempting. It was still dark outside which made the shop look even cosier and more inviting.

Finally. The moment had come where she could stand back and feel proud of what she'd achieved. What she and Gudrun had achieved. This store meant more to Rachel than any of the others because she had been there every step of the way. It meant more than any of the other stores because of where it was and where it had taken her. It had brought her to this amazing place that had changed her life.

At the moment she was wavering over whether her life really was going to be better than it had been before; that hope had gone for the moment because despite her and Jonas deciding that they didn't need to think about the future, she had been. And now those tiny little beginnings of thinking of a future that involved Jonas had gone. She tried to pin down where she had thought this future would be? She'd never expected that he would want to leave Iceland...Had she been thinking of herself in Iceland? Could she do that? That was a bigger question and a moot point now that Jonas had ended things, but Rachel knew she was going to be different. She would go back to a different kind of life and she was glad about that. Feeling the cold begin to pinch at her ears, she went back inside.

At five minutes to nine Gudrun gathered everyone around the kitchen island, Rachel was desperate for a coffee because it smelt so good, but they weren't allowed any yet. There was already a small queue of people outside which was impressive for this hour on a dark Saturday morning.

"Thank you all for your hard work," began Gudrun, "you've made the store look amazing for today. Remember, don't be afraid to approach people, smile, ask if you're not sure about anything and most of all have fun."

They all clapped and then she went over to the door, flicked the latch and opened it, saying what the English people assumed to be "Welcome to Snug" in Icelandic and they were open.

Now that the shop was finished Rachel was forced to abandon the window sofa for fear of looking like part of the display so she lingered near the coffee machine for most of the morning moving occasionally to show someone the best place to put something or to help bring some of the extra stock upstairs. She couldn't stop looking at her favourite item which was a lampshade that looked like the Northern Lights when it had a bulb inside it. She'd never seen anything like it. It had a clever double-layered shade and the inner one rotated slowly making the shimmering waves on the outer layer. There were also pinpricks all over it which looked like stars. It was beautiful, and later that day she could resist it no longer and put one aside for herself as a souvenir of her trip. Despite not having seen the Northern Lights, the thought of them and the lampshade would always make her think of Jonas.

The day went by in the blink of an eye, as it always does when you are busy. There was a steady stream of customers all day and at times, there seemed to be barely room for another person in the store. Despite that, it looked tidy and well-stocked and the flow of the store seemed to be working to keep people moving around.

When the doors closed at 6 pm the several people still in the shop were released by Gudrun who was manning the door now, once they'd finished browsing or buying.

"How do you think the first day went?" Rachel asked her as they waited for the last couple of people to pay.

"It was *amazing*. Do you think so?"

"I don't think it can have gone better," Rachel said, and they hugged. "Congratulations!"

"Rachel, I haven't had a chance to say thank you for everything. I couldn't have done it without you and I'll miss you so much. Why don't you stay here and work for me?"

Rachel laughed but could tell by Gudrun's face that she wasn't joking.

"That is a tempting offer but I think Luisa would have something to say about that. I will come back and visit though because I love it here. You know that."

"I know what you're leaving behind Rachel. Did you go and see him?"

"Yes, we said goodbye." Rachel's eyes filled with tears and she smiled and attempted to blink them away. "And you know that already. I'm sure Olafur told you I saw him afterwards."

Gudrun looked slightly sheepish. "Yes, he did but Jonas hasn't said a word about it. I need more information."

"Come on, lock the door because we need to cash up."

It was a ritual with every store opening that everyone stayed behind to cash up. Normally it was just the store manager who would deal with the money but on the first day, everyone was allowed to know. Gudrun stood behind the counter with Julia running the end-of-day procedure. They grinned and looked at each other.

"Seven hundred and eleven thousand Krona!" Gudrun announced as she waved the strip of paper over her head. Everyone cheered and Julia produced a bottle of champagne and some plastic champagne flutes.

"To Snug Reykjavik!" they all chanted, followed by a "Skål!"

Rachel had seen Adam earlier when he called into the shop briefly to see Julia but she had mercifully been too busy to talk to him at that point. She thought he must have gone back to London because otherwise he probably would have shown up at closing time. She had nothing to say to him anyway and was drained just thinking about what awaited at home.

Dave and Julia had booked a table at the hotel for dinner. Gudrun went home and was going to meet them at the hotel later. Rachel went up to her room and for the first time in days, felt like she could relax.

She lay there, thinking about Jonas. How was he doing, she wondered. She'd be able to ask Gudrun later. Had he asked about her or was she completely out of his thoughts now that she was about to leave and their... whatever it was, was over. No, she remembered Gudrun had been fishing for information. Maybe he hadn't said anything. She had to try and put it behind her. Gudrun's offer of a job had been playing on her mind as well. In reality, there was no way she could work for Gudrun, she needed more of a challenge than that, but the idea of staying in Iceland hugely appealed and it was the first time she had seriously considered it as a possibility. A germ of an idea had been niggling at her since she had met Eldey with the beautiful blankets at the Design Call. It needed to percolate a bit more, but Rachel was excited.

It had been a couple of days since she'd checked her emails properly; as Luisa had arrived it wasn't necessary. There was lots of rubbish to trawl through as usual with the only ones of interest being from her brother asking if she had bought anything for their dad's birthday and if so could he go halves, and there was a message from Adam. Sent today.

Rachel, I didn't think there was anything else to say to each other at the moment so thought to keep things on a professional level I wouldn't approach you to say goodbye today in the shop. I'm glad things went well with the opening and despite

everything, I am looking forward to seeing you when you come home. Adam x

So, he had gone. It was a huge relief to know that he wasn't going to show up at dinner. It would have been a nightmare with everyone knowing that they'd broken up but yet he was involved in the sale of the business. She shuddered at the thought of Stella giving him the third degree.

Having freshened her make-up and brushed her hair, Rachel went downstairs to meet everyone for dinner. She met Gudrun just as she was arriving in the lobby.

"Oh, *helvetis frystingu!*" she said, pulling off her hat and mitts.

"I take it it's cold?" Rachel guessed.

Gudrun sat down on one of the sofas and removed her snow boots switching them for some chunky black Mary Janes. Rachel perched next to her.

"How's Jonas?"

"A little better this evening. He is turning from 'in pain' grumpy to just plain grumpy so we think that is a good sign. But seriously, he looks more colourful."

Rachel smiled at Gudrun's expression and because she was glad to hear he was starting to look better.

"That's good. Will you say I asked after him? Actually, don't. We said goodbye, I'm sure he can do without me going on."

"Rachel, it wasn't because he doesn't love you. You do know that, don't you?" She paused. "He can't see a way forward, that's all. And it was bad timing with his accident. The way he felt before, it hasn't changed."

"It's too late now, Gudrun. I can't go to him again now, it was too hard to leave before. And I can't offer a way forward either." She wasn't ready to share her idea with Gudrun and risk Jonas finding out that she was thinking about a way to stay. One thing was clear to Rachel, this was her decision with or without Jonas, not because of him. If she'd learned anything from the past few weeks it was that she had to be in charge of her own destiny and meandering alongside someone while they were on the way to their's, wasn't the way forward for her anymore.

"What will be will be," said Gudrun wisely and slightly oddly, Rachel thought. "Ready?" She took Rachel's hand and pulled her up from the sofa.

32

The next day Rachel languished in bed, allowing herself a little lie-in which was fine as long as she was at the shop for 11 am. Her last full day in Iceland. How different she felt from when she had arrived just a few weeks ago. It felt like she'd been away for months. Now that she was almost leaving, she let thoughts of returning to London into her mind, thoughts which she'd been actively ignoring for days and days. What was she going to do? Where was she going to go? She couldn't go back to the loft as if nothing had happened and even if Adam would have her there, she knew it would be horrible living together. There was only one bed for a start. No, she had to face the future and make a plan.

"Christ, Rachel, it's only 10 am here. And it's Sunday. What fricking time is it in Iceland?"

It hadn't occurred to Rachel that it would be too early to call Anna.

"It's the same time, but it's an emergency."

"I'm in London, Rach. Not much use to you in an emergency at the moment."

"Can I stay with you for a few days when I get back? I'm flying in tomorrow morning."

"Oh my God, you're actually coming back? Somehow I thought that Icelandic man might have swept you off your feet and I'd never see you again. Of course, you can stay as long as you like."

"Thanks, Anna. I'll go to the loft and pick some things up and then be round late afternoon."

"Perfect. I'm in all day, working from home. See you whenever, I'll have the wine ready and you can tell me everything."

Well, that was the first immediate problem solved. Everything else could wait.

*

On her way to the shop, Rachel picked up coffee and pastries from Te & Kaffi for the last time. The shop was open but quiet when she arrived so she and Gudrun sat at the kitchen island with their coffee while the other two staff chatted and tidied the shelves.

"So, tonight is your last night?" asked Gudrun.

"Yep. Last day in the shop today."

"I have a plan. It is the last chance for you to see the aurora. Olafur checked and the forecast is good so shall we drive outside the city and see if we are lucky?"

"That sounds like a great idea," said Rachel enthusiastically. "Just the two of us?" Maybe Olafur and Jonas were going to tag along.

"Yes, Jonas can't go anywhere and Olafur has to work," she replied, reading Rachel's mind.

"No, that's fine. Thanks, Gudrun. It'll be brilliant to do something like that before I go."

"And bring your swimming costume because I have a cool place to show you on the way."

"Do you have the folder for the Design Call handy? I just wanted to check something."

"It's on the desk in the office. Help yourself."

Rachel leafed through the folder until she found Eldey's details. She pulled out her phone and punched her number in.

"Eldey? It's Rachel from the Snug store. I have an idea to run past you if you don't mind?"

*

After work, Rachel waited outside the hotel with her swimming kit as instructed and she didn't have to wait long before Gudrun came along to pick her up. It was already dark and Rachel knew she would spend most of the evening looking upwards because the skies looked clear.

"You have your swimming things?" Gudrun asked, looking at her bag.

"Yes, all set."

"Great! Olafur just checked the aurora forecast to see where we should head after our swimming for the best chances. There are good predictions for tonight, we should be lucky," she smiled.

"Thanks for organising this, Gudrun. I've been so desperate to see the Northern Lights and I thought I'd missed my chance."

"No problem. It's a pleasure. It's a nice way to say goodbye. And I do think we'll be lucky but you never know with the aurora."

"So where are we going first? Is it a swimming pool?' asked Rachel.

"I want it to be a surprise because you have to see it to believe it, I can't explain." She was shaking her head and grinning so enthusiastically that it made Rachel laugh.

"Oh, Gudrun, I will miss you!" She had never struck up such a good relationship with anyone she'd worked with before and she would be sorry to leave that behind.

"What will you do when you go home? I suppose you won't go back to live with Adam?"

"No, I'll pick some stuff up then I'm going to stay with my friend Anna for a few days. Can you imagine how awful it would be?" Rachel shuddered.

"Pretty awful. Have you spoken to him since he left?"

"No. I sent him an email to say that I'd be staying with Anna but he's not replied."

"I still can't believe he came here about the Snug takeover without telling you. Olafur and I tell each other everything, even secrets. You should be able to keep each other's secrets when you are partners."

"He was always quite secretive about work. I suppose his job does depend on that sometimes and I never minded that he didn't tell me. But you're right. It was strange and quite embarrassing that he would have come here without at least mentioning that he was here for work, even if he wasn't going to tell me it was to do with Snug. But I suppose that was because I'd broken up with him. He was probably trying to get the upper hand to make himself feel better."

"He probably needed to show you that he was in control of something. It is a little childish but I think men can get that way when their ego is bruised."

"Are we there?" Rachel asked as they took a turning off the main road.

"Almost. It is called the Secret Lagoon and it's really hard to find unless you know where to look. Even Olafur used to get lost when he led excursions here."

They did indeed seem to be in the middle of nowhere. There were very few buildings although unusually there were quite a few trees along the side of the road. There are hardly any trees in Iceland because the Vikings used them all up for building, a fact Rachel had learned from Jonas.

The track came to an end in an open area where Gudrun parked the car, next to a low stone building. There were no other cars at all and it seemed completely deserted.

"It looks closed," said Rachel.

"It is closed. A friend of Olafur's owns it and he is letting us visit specially by ourselves."

"That's so cool! What a treat."

They went into a foyer, all the walls inside were stone too. It was very dimly lit but Gudrun led the way to the changing rooms. They took a cubicle each and Rachel had barely started taking her clothes off before Gudrun shouted, "I'll see you in there!"

The changing rooms led onto a long corridor which again was barely lit but Rachel could see the darkness at the end and she could feel the cold air coming in as there seemed to be no door at the end. She walked rapidly towards the outdoors because it was absolutely freezing. The slate tiled floor turned into wooden slatted decking just before the end of the corridor and she could see the dark ripple of the water and wooden steps leading down into it. As she emerged into the icy darkness all Rachel could think of was immersing herself in the warm water. It was like stepping into a hot bath, almost hotter than she thought she could bear; it was complete bliss.

Once her eyes had adjusted to the darkness, she could make out how clear the water was. She swam out a couple of strokes to look for Gudrun. She could just see her, further into the pool, so she lazily swam over to meet her.

"Hey Gudrun!" she called and saw her raise her hand into the darkness in response. Rachel headed over slowly, languishing in the incredible warmth and marvelling at how amazing it was to be outside in this surprising place. On the edge of the pool further over towards Gudrun were lots of jars with candles in, shedding just enough light for Rachel to see the shape of the pool more clearly. It appeared to be completely natural because she could make out the shapes of rocks around the sides and she could feel with her feet that the bottom was shingle and stone.

As she swam towards Gudrun, she noticed that – it wasn't Gudrun after all. This person was broader, fairer and without wishing to offend Gudrun, exactly the person Rachel would want to be with in a place like this.

33

"Jonas! Oh my God! What are you doing here?"

He reached out his hand and gently pulled Rachel nearer to him, kissing her before he said anything to explain himself.

"Oh, look at your poor shoulder, are you even allowed to come swimming?"

"I'm not swimming," he said, continuing to kiss her.

It was so wonderful to see him again, Rachel felt like she was fizzing all over. His kisses were making her weak at the knees but she had a hundred questions about why he was there. Had he changed his mind? Wasn't it too late? What did he think was going to happen now?

"Jonas…" She didn't want to break the spell but… "Really," she said gently, "what are you doing here?"

"I made a mistake, Rachel. It was a mistake to say goodbye to you, to let you go. I don't know what I was thinking but I was hurting and I was afraid of how I felt about you. I wanted to try to stop myself from falling for you when you were going to leave. But it was too late and I hadn't realised that I had completely fallen in love with you until I had said goodbye. I'm so sorry. I said it so that neither of us would get hurt but look what happened. But I have had a couple of days to think, I have had nothing else to do." He gestured to his shoulder which was in a very wet sling but visible enough for Rachel to see that it was black and blue. "I can come to London -"

"No, you couldn't Jonas. It's part of you and I can't imagine you being anywhere else. You wouldn't be happy and your business is here. But I could leave England."

As she said it aloud, she realised she wasn't just saying it because Jonas had offered the same, she had already made up her mind. After all, what was she going back to? Not Adam anymore and maybe not Snug, at least not as she knew it. "I could stay here." Her eyes widened as she could suddenly see that there could be a future or them. "I have an idea for a business. I might need your help to start it off but I want to stay and I think I've found a way to make it happen."

Strangely, it had crossed her mind before that she could stay but she'd struggled with the idea of leaving her job almost to the point where she had not considered it possible. She loved her job, it was a big part of her life, had been almost her whole life when she'd been in London. But that wasn't what mattered anymore. Maybe it was the uncertainty of what might happen to Snug now that had jolted her out of thinking that she couldn't leave it behind but there were other things now that were more important. What mattered was Jonas, life, love, the people she loved and she felt a huge sense of euphoria at being able to grab hold of that now with no regrets and all the excitement of embarking on a new adventure that just a few weeks ago she would never have thought possible.

"Rachel, are you sure? I am happy to come to London with you. I can't ask you to leave everything and come here."

"You didn't ask me, Jonas, I decided and nothing will change my mind. When I thought you didn't want us to be together, when we said goodbye, I couldn't imagine what I was going to do but now I know. And you want that too..." She looked at his troubled expression and was crestfallen. "Oh, that's not what you meant."

"I just want you to be happy, Rachel. It's a huge decision... you must think about it for a few days. Go home and see how you feel then."

"I am going home but just to tidy up all the loose ends so that I can come back and be with you. I don't need any time to think things over. I've spent the past two weeks knowing that all I want to do is be with you and since I saw you at Gudrun's house, well it really made me think about what I want and what the most important things in my life are. And basically, they're all you. I'm staying."

She jumped upright out of the water and landed with a huge splash on her back. "I'm moving to Iceland!" she shrieked before disappearing under the water.

Jonas laughed at her from the side of the pool.

Gudrun and Olafur appeared in their swimming things clutching beers for all of them. They ran along the edge of the pool, put the beers down next to Jonas and then leapt in.

"She's staying!" announced Jonas, still laughing at Rachel who had emerged and was now hugging Gudrun.

"Thank goodness for that," said Olafur. "We couldn't stand another minute of looking at your sad little face," he said, tickling Jonas under the chin.

"Get off, *halfviti!*" said Jonas, pushing Olafur away good-naturedly. Rachel and Gudrun swam back to the side of the pool and they all grabbed a beer.

"Skál!" They clinked their bottles with each other and settled in a row leaning against the rocky edge of the pool, looking up at the clear, starry night. The extraordinary darkness meant that there were so many more stars than Rachel had ever seen before.

"I wouldn't want to be anywhere else tonight. It's magical here."

Then as she kept looking, she could see waves of green in the sky. Or was it her imagination? She'd waited so long to see the aurora borealis that she thought her mind might have been playing tricks - wanting to make the night as perfect as possible. But as she kept her eyes skywards, the glimpses of the waves turned from a hint of colour into a huge ribbon of green and purple shimmering across the sky right in front of her.

"Look! It's happening! I never thought I'd see them, it's beautiful," she said, with tears in her eyes.

Looking at Jonas and seeing that he was having the same reaction as her, was the most perfect and amazing moment. She pressed herself against him and he wrapped his arm around her shoulders and pulled her in tight as they watched the spectacle.

"You're beautiful," he whispered. "Rachel, if you are going to stay I need to make a promise to you. I promise to love you and look after you every day."

Nothing else he could have said at that moment would have been more perfect.

"I promise that to you too," she said solemnly. She put her arm around his neck and pulled him to her; her turn to kiss him. "I couldn't love you more than I do at this minute."

"Drink your beer," he said with a grin. Rachel looked down at her bottle and could see something sparkling in the candlelight. There was a ring tied on a piece of ribbon which had been slipped over the neck of the bottle. Rachel looked at Jonas in disbelief as he took the ring and placed it on her finger, ribbon and all.

"You don't have to propose to make me want to stay."

"It's maybe not a proposal, a promise of a future together. For now."

"It's perfect. I love you, Jonas."

"I love you too, Rachel. Here's to us. Skál!"

The End

Note from the Author

Thank you so much for choosing to read Snug in Iceland, I hope you enjoyed it. If you did, I would be so grateful if you were able to leave a review on Amazon. It makes a huge difference to authors, something I didn't realise until I was one.

I started writing this story after a trip to Iceland for my fortieth birthday. Whether it was because it was our first real weekend away without our kids or whether it's because it's so different to the UK, I don't really know, but it felt magical. I'd always wanted to write a novel and Reykjavik gave me the inspiration I needed although it took a long time to become the book you've just read. My friend Kate and my mum were early readers who were very kind about the fact that Rachel ended up staying with Adam, instead of screaming at me that that was not what was supposed to happen. Eventually, I worked it out for myself and found Rachel and Jonas's story and their happy ever after.

Lots of people have helped me get Snug in Iceland out into the world. My friend Catherine Bowdler introduced me to the Romantic Novelists' Association and suggested I went to my first conference which was terrifying and brilliant at the same time. Thanks to Bernadette and Mick for rescuing me from a lonely coffee break at that first conference and introducing me to the RNA Birmingham Chapter and Michele, Ellie, Helen, Pippa and everyone else there who makes it such a wonderful group to be part of. Thank you to Berni Stevens for taking the cover design I had in my head and making it a reality and for helping me navigate the world of KDP. Thanks to Catrin for doing the most brilliant job of proofreading and agreeing to payment in cocktails.

And lastly James, Jake and Claudia. Thank you for reading this book and loving it. Or at least telling me that you did. As well as it being for Nanny and Grandad, it's for you - a reminder of one of the best family holidays we've had.

Printed in Great Britain
by Amazon